D1308080

Up in Flames!

Stephen E. Stanley

Jeremy's 1936 Cadillac

Up in Flames

© 2013 Stephen E. Stanley
All rights reserved.

ISBN-10: 1484130065
ISBN-13: 978-1484130063

Printed in the United States of America.

Stonefield Publishing 2013

Author's Note:

This book is a work of fiction. All characters, names, institutions, and situations depicted in the book are the product of my imagination and not based on any persons living or dead. Anyone who thinks he or she is depicted in the book is most likely delusional and should be institutionalized.

Stonefield Publishing
Portland, Maine
StonefieldPublishing@gmail.com

Author's Web page: http://stephenestanley.com/

Up in Flames!

A Jeremy Dance Mystery

Stephen E. Stanley

Preface

Historically speaking the 1930s presented a time of challenge and change. Almost one quarter of American workers were unemployed, while the top two percent of Americans enjoyed a level of prosperity that was unchanged from the previous decades.

Race relations, too was about to change. Depictions of African Americans in popular culture presented the country with stereotypes portraying blacks as servile and simpleminded, while in reality the movement toward civil rights was well underway. The flowering of the Harlem Renaissance and establishment of the American Negro Congress in 1936 and the growing voice of the NAACP began the slow march to the civil rights movement of the 1960s.

Gay and lesbians, on the other hand, were facing a society that was becoming more and more conservative. The liberalism of the 1920s that allowed GLBT persons to be more or less open now began to face a growing world of hostility and persecution.

All of this makes a fascinating background in which to place fictional characters. I've tried to incorporate these various elements as the background in the Jeremy Dance mysteries, but I make no claim to historical accuracy.

The crimes in this book are based on real crimes that happened in the early twentieth century, but again there is no claim to accuracy as this is a book of fiction, and I have changed many elements to fit the plot.

Finally, I write the types of stories I like to read. It is a joy to write and my hope is that you, the reader, will like them, too.

Stephen E. Stanley

Cast of Characters

Jeremy Dance—Jeremy is young, rich, and very good at restoring lost things.

Judy Hogarth—Jeremy's best friend and a young Back Bay socialite.

Robert Williams—an heir to a popular canned meat business, Rob prefers to live simply as a homicide detective for the Boston Police.

Roscoe Jackson—a gentleman of color, Roscoe is Jeremy's right hand man.

Velda Dance—Jeremy's twin sister and an artist in her own right.

Lyle Compton—Manger of the Windsor Club.

Father James Morrison—rector of St Martin's Church.

Emma Goodwin—grand dame of Beacon Hill. Emma is a fountain of information.

Jimmy Kirk—Jeremy's chef.

Nora Wilde—suspects her father's fiancé may be dangerous.

Ina Patterson—seems to have bad luck with husbands.

Myra Pennington—former social columnist, Myra is now a Washington reporter with a national following.

David Hopper—hires Jeremy to help him save his job.

Mark Johnson—accountant at Brigham Financial Services.

Cora Andrews—hires Jeremy to find her missing husband.

Ken McKenzie—police detective in Niagara Falls, NY.

Julie Patterson—owner of Island Real Estate in Bar Harbor.

I would like to thank Stonefield Publishing for taking a chance on an unknown writer. Small publishers such as Stonefield do not have the resources that big publishing companies have and do not have a full-time staff of copyreaders. Any typos or omissions are strictly my own. I would also like to thank my partner Raymond Brooks for his continued support and dog sitting skills.

Stephen E. Stanley 2013

Love is a fire. But whether it is going to warm your hearth or burn your house down, you can never tell. --Joan Crawford

Chapter 1

It was raining on Beacon Hill, but then June tends to be a rainy month, and 1936 was proving to be a rainy year so far. The whole effect of the weather had been to cast a gloomy atmosphere that had seemed to hover over Boston for days. If the sun doesn't come out soon, I thought darkly, the murder rate in the city will climb. Jeremy Dance Restorations provides a wide range of services, and thankfully murder investigations are rare.

Jeremy Dance Restorations is a business I started out of my Beacon Hill townhouse. My clients come to me by word-of-mouth and I provide a wide range of services. When Grandma wanders off and disappears, they call me. When the maid pockets some expensive jewels, I'm the one they hire. When junior at college has one too many and disappears, I'm on the case. The upper crust of Boston likes to keep their secrets and they know that I offer quality service and discretion.

My personal life is something else, however. To put it bluntly my Philadelphia family has more money than the Vatican. My mother died some years and left me and my sister to the mercy of my stepmother whom we both loath. My sister took the lead and we both adopted my mother's maiden

1

name and moved away, and took a huge chunk of the family fortune with us.

Mostly I work alone with the help of my assistant, Roscoe Jackson. At times I'm helped by my "special friend" and former classmate police lieutenant Rob Williams.

I was hoping for an easy summer. I had been busy working on several cases for most of the winter and I had only been able to get away to someplace warm for a few weeks. I vowed that this summer I would get away to my hideout in the mountains.

"Gentleman to see you, Mr. Jeremy," said Roscoe Jackson, interrupting my thoughts. Roscoe Jackson is my right hand man. Cook, driver, valet, and investigator, I couldn't manage without his help.

"Show him in, Roscoe."

Roscoe reappeared with a young man of average height, somewhere in his early twenties. His suit, though fashionable and neatly pressed, was obviously from a department store. With dark curly hair and glasses, he struck me as a businessman. I stood up to introduce myself.

"Welcome, I'm Jeremy Dance. How may I be of service?"

"My name is David Hopper. I'm with Brigham Financial Services, and I need your help."

"Have a seat Mr. Hopper. This is Mr. Jackson. He'll be taking notes." The three of us sat down in the small seating area of my study. "Now, tell me why you think you need my help."

"I'm about to be fired."

"I'm not sure I can help you with that, Mr. Hopper."

"It wasn't my fault."

"Maybe you need to start at the beginning," I suggested. I looked at the clock on the mantle and wondered briefly how long this was going to take. Employment issues weren't in my realm of talents.

"It happened last week. My boss gave me an assignment. I was to take a collection of bonds and important papers and deliver them to the New York office. They were placed in a sealed package and given to me. I took the train and I swear they were never out of my sight."

"I take it the package disappeared?"

"No, that's just it. I delivered the package."

"And?"

"And when it was opened it was full of cut up newspapers. There were no certificates."

"I see," I said. "Did you see the certificates being placed in the package?"

"Yes, I was there in the office when they made up the package."

"Did they accuse you of stealing them?"

"No, not exactly."

"What do you mean?"

"They accused me of being careless. They said I must have been the victim of a thief. He must have bumped into me and switched the packages in the confusion."

"Could that have happened?"

"I guess. How else can you explain it?"

"What would you like me to do?" I asked.

"I'd like you to find the missing papers."

"I'm sure your company has insurance."

"It's a matter of trust. You see the company is owned by my uncle. His two partners didn't want to hire me, but my uncle went out on a limb, and now I've let him down. I'm sure they'll use this as an excuse to get rid of me."

"My services," I said, "are not cheap."

"Will this be enough of a retainer?" said David Hopper as he passed me a check already made out to me.

"Yes," I said looking at the amount. "That should be more than enough to get started."

"Thank you for taking the case, Mr. Dance," he said as he got up to leave. "Here's my card. Let me know when you find out anything."

"Mr. David Hopper," I said to Roscoe after the young man left, "is not who he appears to be."

Judy Hogarth cupped her hands around a cup of tea as we sat in the little café on Arlington Street. We had just walked across the Boston Common and through the Public Gardens. The rain had cleared and it was a picture perfect day. The swan boats were gliding back and forth on the water giving some fluid movement to the sleepy scene.

"You really should find something useful to do," I said to Judy. "Being a socialite in 1936 doesn't exactly advance the human cause."

"I know," she answered grimly. "I'm just not really good at anything."

"Nonsense. You've helped me out in my investigations many times. It's just that you need to have something to get up for in the morning. How about charity work?"

"Charity work?" I could see her thinking it over. "Maybe. You think there is anything to do?"

"Look around. There are thousands out of work. People don't have enough to eat. Of course there are things to do." I love Judy like a sister, but she's not terribly aware of goings on outside of her social class.

"I wouldn't even know where to start."

"Let's see," I said. I thought it over for a moment. "Father Morrison is organizing a soup and bread line down at St. Martin's. I'm sure he could use some help. You could even get some of your society friends to help out."

"St. Martin's? How many poor Episcopalians are out there?"

"More than you think. The depression has hit everyone. But the food program is for anyone in need, not just church goers."

"Okay, maybe I'll call on Father Morrison and see what I can do."

"I think you should. Have you heard from Myra?" Myra Pennington is a reporter for the

Boston Post. She and Judy are, to put in bluntly, lovers. Being outside the boundaries of society is something that we both share.

"She's been assigned to Washington to cover the new president and his plans to get the country out of this depression. I don't know when I'll see her."

"Well it certainly is a boost to her career. Six months ago she was a society columnist writing about dinner parties that no one cared about."

"Yes, thanks to you. I don't know whether to be grateful to you or angry."

"Let's go with the grateful."

"Speaking of romance, I haven't seen Robert around very much."

"No," I sighed. "Robert is still with the police. The insurance investigator job didn't pan out. He missed the excitement of police work."

"But he's rich; he doesn't have to work."

"Some misguided people just like to work."

"I suppose," said Judy, not really believing it.

Brigham Financial Services has offices down on Milk Street. The stone art deco building was recently constructed and appears more ornate than the surrounding buildings. The fact that they could afford to build a new building during this depression suggested that they were financially solid. I had called ahead and made an appointment with David Hopper's supervisor.

While I'm not usually a fan of modern furnishings, I was impressed with the lobby of the building. Three of the walls were covered with huge murals in earth tones and the reception area was colorful without being garish. It took two receptionists to handle both the desk and the switchboard.

"May I help you?" asked the first receptionist. She was dressed in a simple black skirt and an ornate white blouse with large, frilly lapels. Her blonde hair was bobbed and Marcel waved, and she wore a fresh gardenia on her blouse.

"I have an appointment with Mr. Chambers."

"You must be Mr. Dance. Marie will show you up." She pressed a button on a large wooden console and a young lady appeared. The receptionist spoke to her briefly and I followed her to the elevator.

"Sixth floor, please," she said to the elevator operator. I was led to an office that had a great view of the custom house tower and the waterfront. Brad Chambers stood up when I entered. Marie introduced us and then left the office. Brad Chambers was what I called a gray man. Somewhere in his fifties or sixties with gray hair and glasses, he was dressed in an impeccable gray suit.

"I understand that David hired you to look into the missing papers."

"Yes, that's correct. I'm afraid David thinks he'll be blamed for being careless and will be fired."

"Blamed, yes, but I doubt that he'll be fired. You see he's engaged to the daughter of John Eagleton, who is the president of the company, not to mention that his uncle is the major stock holder."

"Mr. Hopper seems to have omitted that part of the story. Still he seemed sincere about clearing his name."

"Yes, I'm afraid he took it very hard and was afraid he'd be blamed for stealing the papers. No one for a minute thought that, but everyone thought he probably wasn't as careful with the papers as he should have been."

"I see. Could you please tell me what you saw when he was given the package?"

"David and I went into Mark Johnson's office. He is the chief accountant. He gave us the papers to examine and then he placed them in a small black portfolio, and then he passed it to David."

"You saw the papers go into the portfolio?"

"Yes."

"And you examined them?"

"Yes."

"Is it usually your job to examine financial papers when they leave the office?"

"No, not really."

"Did you think it strange that you were asked to examine the bonds this time?"

"No. I just assumed it was because it was a larger than usual transfer."

"I see. Would it be possible for me to speak to this Mr. Johnson?"

"I'm afraid Mr. Johnson is on vacation for a few weeks. He's due back next week."

"Thank you for your time Mr. Chambers."

"I hope you can help David. We really are all very fond of him."

"I'll do my best," I promised. I just hoped I was up for the task.

Chapter 2

Roscoe brought me a steaming cup of coffee along with the morning paper. The day promised to be bright and sunny and I was contemplating taking a day off and driving up to my camp in the White Mountains. I only had the Hopper case to work on and there wasn't much I could do until the accountant, Mark Johnson, returned from vacation. I was hoping I could convince Robert Williams to go with me. Rob is a homicide detective with the Boston police.

Rob had to be careful to keep his private life under wraps because of his job. For a brief time he had contemplated leaving the department to become an insurance investigator, but when he received a department award for his work on a murder case last winter, he had decided to stay with the department for a few more months. I had just opened the newspaper when Roscoe came back into the room.

"Lady to see you Mr. Jeremy," he said.

I looked at the clock and sighed. It was only eight-thirty. I knew that my plans for the White Mountains would have to wait. "Better show her in, Roscoe."

"Good morning, Mr. Dance," said the auburn haired young lady. She was wearing a stylish dress, and she was neatly coiffed. She held herself with much understated elegance, and I guessed her to come from old money. "I'm Nora Wilde."

"Pleased to meet you Miss Wilde. Please have a seat and tell me how I can help you." She took a seat in the red leather chair across from my desk. "Would you like some coffee?"

"That would be most kind, thank you." Roscoe poured her a cup from the carafe. I motioned to him to sit down. He pulled out a pad of paper and prepared to take notes.

"Mr. Jackson is my assistant and will be taking notes," I explained as she looked in his direction. She nodded.

"I understand that you do discrete inquiries?"

"Yes, that's true, if a case interests me. I don't advertise, so I'm curious how you found me."

"I met your sister Velda at a party. She suggested that you might be able to help."

"My services come with a price, Miss Wilde."

"Money is not a problem, Mr. Dance."

"You better tell me all about it."

"I'm afraid that everyone in society knows about my problem," she sighed. "You see, my mother died two years ago. My father worshipped the ground she walked on and was totally lost. Then he became involved with Ina Patterson. Ina quickly latched onto my father and he, being lost and lonely, was only too willing to let her control his life. It's no secret that Ina despises me. Now he plans to marry her."

"Miss Wilde, I should tell you that I don't usually handle domestic disputes."

11

"I understand that, Mr. Dance, but I fear that my father is in danger."

"Danger?"

"Yes, you see Ina is a widow."

"I'm afraid I don't see the danger in that."

"She's been married three times. Each of her husbands has died within a few years of marriage. All three are reputed to have been healthy and each died suddenly."

Roscoe closed his notebook and sat up. I looked at him and he nodded.

"We'll take the case, Miss Wilde."

Jimmy Kirk placed a plate of sandwiches on my desk. Jimmy rounds out my all male household. I hired him to take over some of the domestic duties when I elevated Roscoe to investigator. As a gentleman of color, Roscoe could go places I couldn't. And though I want to punch people in the face when they say something like "they all look alike," society's prejudice had rendered Roscoe almost invisible. Most white people wouldn't be able to pick him out of a lineup, and this made for a good detective.

"How's Jimmy working out?" asked Rob Williams once Jimmy was out of the room. Rob had joined me for lunch. He had the morning off and didn't have to report to the department until late afternoon.

"Roscoe's done a good job of training him. Jimmy is always in motion doing something."

"Where is Roscoe?"

"I gave him the afternoon off. And Jimmy will be leaving as well, which means we have a good two hours and the house to ourselves."

"What shall we do with the time?" asked Rob with a wicked smile.

"Eat your sandwich," I said. "I have a few ideas."

Emma Goodwin sat primly on the edge of her chair in the drawing room of her Mt. Vernon Street home. She held a saucer in one hand and a dainty teacup in the other. I had a rather larger cup of coffee in my hand. I detest tea and most of the better homes in Boston serve both coffee and tea during calling hours.

"It's kind of you to visit with me, Jeremy, though I suspect you're looking for information as usual."

"I always enjoy your company," I protested. "But of course if you could share some information with me, I'd be most appreciative." Mrs. Emma Goodwin had lived on Beacon Hill for over sixty years and knew everyone and had a vast arsenal of gossip on everyone. If there were family skeletons, she knew not only where they were buried, but who buried them.

"I'm not one to gossip, you understand. But I know you must be working on a case or you wouldn't be here."

"What can you tell me about Nora Wilde?"

"Nora Wilde?" she said to herself and was quiet for a few moments while she searched her memory. "Ah, yes. Such a tragedy! Her mother was Liddy Osgood before she married Cornelius Wilde. They both came from money, but I understand they detested each other."

"Nora told me that her father worshiped the ground she walked on."

"That, I'm sure, is how she chooses to see it. But everyone else knows better."

"I see." That certainly put a different spin on things.

"Liddy died suddenly on a trip to New York."

"What did she die from?"

"The doctor said it was a heart attack, but she was only forty-five."

"Where did she die?"

"Apparently on the train. When the train pulled into Penn Station she didn't get off. She was dead in her seat."

"That's a rather extreme reaction to New York, don't you think?"

"Dying on the train is certainly not in good taste," remarked Emma with a twinkle in her eye.

"Liddy Osgood? The name seems to ring a bell."

"She and your late mother were classmates at Wellesley."

"Maybe that's where I've heard it," I said trying to think.

"Have you heard from your family? I understand that there is an estrangement." Emma, having supplied me with gossip, was looking for payment in kind. It was a fair trade. My sister Velda and I had disowned our father when he married his second wife. She had urged my father to send me off when Rob and I were involved in a scandal. My stepmother had taken an instant dislike to Velda and Velda, to her credit, loathed the woman.

Our mother left us well off and we didn't need my father's money at all. We are also heirs to the Dance Department Stores that out grandparents founded. Money, needless to say, was never an issue.

"Emma," I said looking at her directly. "You know perfectly well the story. But things are improving somewhat. My father and I have exchanged letters and phone calls, and he wants to come to Boston for a visit. But we've made it clear he has to come alone."

"I don't know what he sees in that woman. But then stepmothers are never well received. I wonder if that's one of the reasons you're taking the Wilde case."

"Maybe; I hadn't thought about it." Could it be that I took the case because I identified with Nora Wilde?

"What do you know about Ina Patterson?" I needed to get focused away from my background.

"Ina Patterson was one of Liddy's best friends. In my opinion she used that fact to advantage when she set her sights on Cornelius."

"What's your opinion of her?" I asked.

"Well, you know me," she began. "I'd rather have my tongue cut out rather than say anything bad about anyone. But Ina Patterson is a witch with a capital B!"

I sat back in my chair momentarily shocked. Emma has strong opinions but is usually more guarded in her conversation.

"I see," was all I could say.

David Hopper sat in the red visitor's chair in my office as I poured us both some coffee from the silver carafe.

"I want you to tell me exactly what happened in the office the day they gave you the package. I want every detail no matter how small or insignificant you think it is."

"I went into Mark Johnson's office with Mr. Chambers. I was given the train ticket for New York. Mr. Johnson explained that I would be delivering certain financial papers to the New York office and that it represented a large sum of money."

"Yes, go on. Did anything unusual happen?"

"No. He took out the papers and explained them to me. He asked Mr. Chambers to double check the papers. He did so and passed them back to Mr. Johnson. He then placed them in the portfolio and sealed them up."

"Did you examine them closely?"

"I saw them, but I didn't read them."

"How come?"

"I wouldn't have known what they were. I don't have anything to do with financial papers."

"I see. What is it exactly that you do at Brigham Financial Services?"

"I study clients' portfolios and write reports and make recommendations for buying and selling."

"Do you work directly with the clients?"

"No, I work with the firm's brokers, who in turn work directly with the clients."

"It must be challenging work in these hard times," I remarked.

"It certainly is. However there are certain stocks that are doing well in spite of the depression."

"Doing well?" I had seen the balance sheets from the Dance Department Store. While the family business was not about to go into bankruptcy, it wasn't making much of a profit.

"I guess it's all relative. We're happy when our clients see any profit in their investments, no matter how small."

A sudden thought struck me. "How is Brigham Financial Services doing?"

"We're able to cover basic expenses and pay salaries, but there hasn't been a profit in two years."

"Was the portfolio you carried insured?

"Oh, yes. I think that's why they didn't fire me. The company won't lose the money."

"Can these financial papers be traded for money?"

"Yes, they are as good as cash. There are no records of the transactions and they can't be traced."

"So you could have stolen them and gotten away with it?"

"I didn't steal them!"

"Relax. I believe you, but others may think otherwise. Do you have any enemies at work?"

"No, not at all. I get along with everyone."

"So," I said getting back to the actual transaction, "tell me what happened next."

"Well, he sealed up the package, as I said before, and then passed it to me."

"Nothing else happened?"

"No... Yes. He dropped it and then picked it up."

"I need to talk to this Mr. Johnson. But I'm pretty confident that I can help you."

Chapter 3

My sister Velda was decked out in a dress in the latest fashion. Velda was a devotee of the Paris fashion world and spent a good deal of her income on clothes. Slowly she sat her coffee cup down on the table and perused the menu.

"We always have good service here," she remarked as she looked around the café.

"That's because our grandparents own this department store."

"The staff here doesn't know that."

"Of course they do. As soon as we walked through the door the sales clerks sent out a warning to everyone. Didn't you notice?"

"No, I guess not, but then I'm not the detective am I?" she remarked. "So what cases are you working on now?"

I gave her a brief outline of the two cases. Normally I don't discuss cases, but of course this was my sister and she knows enough to be discrete.

"Liddy Osgood? I'm sure I've heard the name before."

"Emma Goodwin claims that Liddy was at Wellesley with mother."

"That's probably where I've heard the name. So I'm sure there's something you want me to do."

"I invited you to lunch because you are my sister."

"And?" she added with a smile.

"And I'd like you to see what you can find out about Ina Patterson."

"Are you suggesting that I indulge in gossip with my Beacon Hill friends?"

"Of course I am."

"It shall be done," she said as the waitress brought our sandwiches.

After lunch I headed over to police headquarters to see Rob Williams. I had called ahead to make sure he was there. The officer at the desk ushered me into the detective division. It was a large room with about a half dozen gray steel desks. Rob waved me over to an empty chair by his desk in the corner.

"Mr. Dance, how can I help you?" asked Rob loud enough for everyone in the room to hear.

I explained what I had figured out about the missing financial papers that David Hopper had been accused of losing."

"So it was a theft?

"Oh yes. A crime has been committed."

"You're sure?" he asked.

"Yes, it's the only explanation. I'd like you to come along when I make my report."

"I certainly will," said Rob.

I called ahead to Brigham Financial Services and arranged for a meeting with David Hopper, Brad Chambers, and John Eagleton, the president of the firm. Mark Johnson was due back, and I thought it was important not to delay. Rob was with me in his capacity as a police detective.

We were seated in a small conference room on the top floor of the building. The view out the windows was amazing. I introduced Rob in his official capacity.

"As you are aware David asked me to look into the missing papers that he was responsible for delivering to the New York office. David swears that the portfolio was never out of his sight. I believe him."

"Then how do you explain that I saw the papers and then saw them placed into the portfolio?" asked Brad Chambers.

"There's nothing to explain. You are correct when you say that the papers were placed in the portfolio, because they were."

"I don't understand," said John Eagleton.

"Where's Mr. Johnson?" I asked. "Wasn't he due back to work today?"

"He was," admitted Brad Chambers, "but he didn't report to work this morning."

"I'm not surprised," I said.

"I don't follow," replied Eagleton.

"What happened after Johnson put the papers in the portfolio?" I asked David.

"He dropped it as he was handing it to me."

"Is that right?" I asked Chambers.

"Yes, now that you mention it, he did drop it."

"I still don't understand," said Eagleton.

"It's very simple," I said. "Johnson asked Mr. Chambers to examine the papers and then placed them in the portfolio. Mr. Chambers here remarked that it was unusual for him to check the papers. That was a clue that something was up. Johnson wanted to make sure that someone could testify that the papers were genuine and that they were in the portfolio."

"So that proves that David had the papers in the portfolio," remarked Eagleton shaking his head.

"Have any of you been to a magic show?" I asked. They all looked at me like I'd lost my mind.

"What has that to do with anything?" asked Chambers.

"Magic is just sleight of hand. Your eyes see what your mind expects to see. Johnson dropped the portfolio and bent over to pick it up. In reality when he stooped to pick it up he switched the portfolio with the real papers with one that was stuffed with newsprint. Johnson stole the papers and left David here to be blamed. I'm not surprised the Johnson skipped work today. I think we better find him before he skips out."

Mark Johnson's apartment building was on Huntington Avenue in the Back Bay section of Boston. The Back Bay had once been marsh land, but had been filled in and built upon with wide, straight avenues that stand in stark contrast to the older sections of Boston with its crooked and winding streets. Rob and I arrived with several police officers to arrest Mark Johnson.

As we headed toward Hunting Avenue from Copley Square we were aware of heavy smoke that was making visibility difficult.

Traffic had been stopped, so we pulled over to a side street and parked the police car. It was only a short walk to the apartment building. As we rounded the corner we saw that a building was engulfed in flames and that fire trucks had arrived and were fighting the fire.

Rob strode over to one of the fireman who was busy organizing some of the other firemen.

"What's going on?"

"A fire started in one of the apartments. We think we got almost everyone out."

I looked at the building number and realized that it was Mark Johnson's apartment building. "Almost everyone?"

"We don't know about the top apartment. That's where the fire started."

"Do you know whose apartment?" I asked, though I already had a feeling I knew.

"Some guy named Johnson," said the fireman as he unwound another reel of hose and headed toward the building.

Back at the police station there was nothing else to do but wait. Rob brought two cups of coffee to his desk and handed me one.

23

"At least you were able to prove that your client was innocent," said Rob stirring cream into his coffee.

"I guess. The question now is where is Mark Johnson and where are the papers he stole?"

"My guess is he disappeared with the portfolio."

"And the fire?"

"A diversion to give him time to escape. He must have known you'd figure out what happened."

"I know. But without a confession we couldn't prove a crime."

"That's true, but it would remove suspicion from David Hopper, which was your goal."

Just then the phone on Rob's desk rang. He picked it up and listened and then set the receiver back down. "That was the chief of police. They found a body in the apartment. It looks like the victim was smoking in bed and fell asleep."

"So it was Mark Johnson?"

"They think so, but the body was burned beyond recognition."

St. Martin's parish was in a poorer section of town. Its congregation made up mostly of workers from different ethnic backgrounds. The depression had affected the neighborhood more than most in the city and the church had become the unofficial meeting place of the community. The parish had been established during better times and fortunately had a large endowment that helped to keep its doors open. The establishment of a bread line was a godsend for the community.

Father James Morrison had set up the breadline two months ago and since then the number of people served had grown steadily since then. I visited the church on occasion and always slipped Father Morrison a check with the understanding that I would remain anonymous.

"Good to see you, Jeremy," said Jim Morrison as I stepped into the parish house kitchen. He had his sleeves rolled up and was stirring a pot of soup on the stove. His wife Jeanine was slicing loaves of bread and smiled at me. I took the check I had written earlier and slipped it into his shirt pocket.

"I can't tell you..." he started to say. I held up my hand to stop him.

"Any fool can write a check," I said.

"But so few do," he laughed.

"I came to check on Judy Hogarth. Is she working out?"

"She's been a huge help," said Jeanine. "She's out there now dishing soup. I'm sure she could use some help."

I slipped out into the parish hall where Judy was standing behind a table and ladling out soup. I was happy to see that she had dressed down for the occasion. The line for soup was long. There were whole families lining up for soup as well as a large number of out of work men. It was heartbreaking to see.

"Need some help?" I asked standing behind her. She spun around to face me.

"Jeremy! Yes, grab a ladle." After about ten minutes the line began to thin.

"How are you doing?" I asked.

"Oh, Jeremy. I never realized how bad things were. We're so lucky."

"Father Morrison says you've been a real help."

"I come here almost every day. It's nice to feel needed."

"I came to invite you to dinner. It'll just be me, Rob, and Velda."

"What time?"

"Around eight."

"I'll be there."

Chapter 4

Rob and I dressed for dinner even though it was an informal affair. I knew Velda would appear in a new frock and Judy would be dressed to the nines. I shot Rob an admiring glance as he stepped out of the shower, dried himself off and slipped into his white dinner jacket.

"How much longer," I asked, "are you going to stay with the police?"

"I like the routine."

"You like the recognition. They lured you back with that citation."

"I can't sit around doing nothing. The insurance investigator job was boring. And look at you. You have tons of money and you'd never have to work if you didn't enjoy it."

"True," I answered. "But I'm my own boss."

"Your tie is crooked." He came over and straightened my tie and kissed me.

"Don't start anything you can't finish."

"I'll get back to you later," he promised with a wink.

Downstairs Roscoe was mixing drinks with the cocktail shaker as I went to the door and greeted Velda and Judy who had arrived at the same time.

"I could sure use this," said Velda as she took the drink from Rob's hand.

"Tough day at the studio?" asked Rob. Velda is an artist and sales had been slow.

"I'm running out of ideas," she replied.

"Time to set up a studio in Maine," I said.

"If the weather ever clears up. It's been raining off and on for two weeks."

"June is always rainy," said Judy. "I can't wait for the warm, dry weather to settle in. I just hope we don't get the hot weather that the Midwest is suffering through."

"Unfortunately," added Rob, "when the hot weather hits, crime in Boston really increases."

"Speaking of crimes," said Velda. "What have you two been up to?"

I gave them the basics of the stolen papers from Brigham Financial Services and how the investigation ended in the fire.

"So the papers are gone up in flames and the man who stole them is dead?" asked Velda.

"It seems that way," said Rob.

"Well," said Judy, "at least you were able to solve the crime."

"I was more interested in clearing my client's name, so I guess it was a success." Something in the back of my mind told me I had missed something, but I couldn't figure out what was bothering me.

Jimmy Kirk appeared and announced that dinner was ready.

I sat at my desk writing out my final report for David Hopper and listing my expenses for the case. His retainer had been more than enough and I was able to write out a check for a refund. I passed my report to Roscoe to type up and mail.

"What are we working on next?" asked Roscoe as he took the report from my hand and placed it on his desk.

"We need to take a look at Ina Patterson. Nora Wilde will want us to investigate her background before Ina manages to marry the father."

"You think she really killed off her husbands?"

"Probably not. Her husbands were all old. Old men die. But at least we can give Miss Wilde peace of mind."

"And if she did kill any of them?"

"Then perhaps we can prevent another murder. I think it's more likely that Nora Wilde doesn't like the idea of someone taking her mother's place, especially since Ina was a friend of her mother's."

"Just goes to show," said Roscoe shaking his head, "that rich people are crazy."

Checking up on Ina Patterson's late husbands wasn't going to be easy. Dead men don't usually give interviews, and I wasn't sure how much information I was going to get from the records. At any rate I was going to be spending time on trains. Ina had three husbands in three different states, which wasn't going to make investigation easy.

The basic facts about Ina were easy enough to get. Ina was born in Philadelphia in 1888 which would make her forty-eight years old. She married her first husband there in 1908. Since I grew up in Philadelphia I was certain I would be able to track down her early life. I had learned that Liddy Osgood and my mother had been classmates with

29

Ina when they were in college. It looked like I'd be visiting Philadelphia, and it wasn't a trip I was looking forward to.

I looked at my watch and saw it was time for lunch. I was meeting Rob at the Windsor Club. The food at the Windsor Club was outstanding and since I had helped solve a murder in the club's back alley, I had been treated by the staff like a king. The all-male enclave was an exclusive and discrete place where men of a certain social class could meet for some privacy.

The weather was pleasant and I decided to walk to the club. The club manager, Lyle Compton, met me at the door and escorted me personally to the dining room, informing me that Mr. Williams had already arrived.

"I hope I'm not late," I said as I took my seat.

"Not at all. I just needed to get away from the station for a few hours."

"What's going on?"

"A murder in Roxbury. Of course no one saw anything or heard anything."

"Neighborhood code of silence?"

"No one is going to testify against the mob."

"It was a professional hit?"

"Looks that way. I hate these crimes. They never get solved."

I looked at him carefully. "You think there are some corrupt cops involved with the mob, don't you?"

"I'm afraid so."

Just then the waiter came over to take our orders. The waiter was new, but very efficient.

"Nice looking waiter," I remarked. "He'll be getting some good tips from the members here."

"He'll be getting more than tips," Rob laughed. "So what are you up to?"

I told him my plan to go to Philadelphia and look into Ina Patterson's past.

"Are you going to see your father while you're there?"

"Not unless I have to," I answered. Rob nodded his head.

"Well before you go running off I have a case for you."

"A case for me? What is it?"

"It's a missing person's case. It seems a woman's husband has disappeared."

"Women's husbands disappear all the time. Usually because they want to disappear."

"I told her the police can look into it, but we don't have the resources and that she'd be better off with a private investigator. I gave her your name."

"What makes you think I'd want this case?"

"Well because there is an interesting twist to the story."

"A twist?" I asked. "What is it?"

"You remember Mark Johnson don't you?"

"Of course. He stole the securities and died in the fire. It was only a few days ago."

"Well, the missing man is his cousin."

31

"That is interesting," I said as our lunch arrived.

"Isn't it?" remarked Rob with a twinkle in his eye.

I really didn't want to take on another case, but since restoration of missing objects was my job, I figured I'd at least listen to the woman who sat in front of me. Roscoe was at his desk quietly taking notes.

"Lieutenant Williams gave me your name and said you were a discrete investigator." Cora Andrews was a woman of middle age immaculately dressed in somber blues and grays. Her eyes had dark circles under them, and I guessed she wasn't sleeping well.

"I've had some success with missing persons, it's true. But not all men who disappear are missing. Many choose to disappear for reasons of their own. You better start at the beginning."

"My husband Dan is a banker with the Cambridge Peoples' Bank. A week ago he left for work. He never showed up at the bank and he never came home."

"And you've had no word from him?"

"No, nothing at all."

"How much money did he have on him?" I could see that the question made her uncomfortable. I watched her struggle for a moment. "If I'm to help you at all you need to tell me everything, even if you think it's not relevant."

"Very well," she answered and looked troubled. "According to the bank he took a substantial amount of money out of our personal account."

"How substantial?"

"Twenty thousand dollars." Roscoe let out a low whistle.

"I see. And when was this?"

"The day before he disappeared."

"So he took out twenty thousand dollars and disappeared the next day and you believe he didn't just run away?"

"Mr. Dance, I know it sounds incredible, but I know my husband, and he would never leave me without an explanation. Do you think you can find him?"

"I'm sure I can find him," I said with more confidence than I felt. "But it will cost a lot of money and there's nothing I can do if he wants to stay lost, unless there is something criminal that he's done."

"Will you take the case? Money is no object."

"Yes, of course. Mr. Jackson here will give you some papers to sign. Please send over a picture of your husband as soon as you can."

"I saw that look in your eye," remarked Roscoe after Cora Andrews left."

"What look?"

"That determined look."

"When?"

"When she said money is no object!" he said and laughed.

"I have to admit, it is one my favorite phrases."

Chapter 5

Roscoe Jackson hovered over us like a mother hen as Rob and I devoured our breakfast. Jimmy Kirk had the day off and Roscoe made and served our breakfast.

"I have vacation time coming up," said Rob as he unfolded the newspaper to check out the headlines. "Where would you like to go?"

"How about Provincetown?"

"That's a great idea. We could rent a house."

"Or Europe for that matter."

"Europe isn't very stable at the moment, but that might work too."

"It won't be for a while. I've got two cases I'm working on at the moment."

"Let's shoot for September," suggested Rob.

"Yes, let's," I said. "I'll keep my case load light."

"What's the plan for today, Mr. Jeremy?" asked Roscoe as he poured us more coffee.

"I'm going to interview Cora Andrews and get some more information. Philadelphia will just have to wait for a few days."

"You think this guy wanted to disappear don't you?" asked Rob.

"He wouldn't be the first man to run out on his wife. I'm sure I can wrap this one up in no time." I wasn't quite as confident as I sounded.

Cora Andrews lived in a quiet section of Cambridge. Roscoe was at the wheel of my yellow

Cadillac as we drove over the Charles River past Central Square and beyond Harvard Yard. The Andrews lived in a neo-classic brick house near Radcliffe College. The neighborhood was much more spacious than the crowded lanes of Beacon Hill.

"This is worlds away from Roxbury," remarked Roscoe as he looked around.

"Lots of money here," I said. "Get your pencil ready, Roscoe. I'm going to try to get the truth out of Mrs. Andrews."

I rang the door bell and a woman of color, dressed as a maid, led us into a well-furnished room. The maid gave Roscoe the once over and appreciation showed in her eyes. "You have an admirer," I said to Roscoe when the maid left the room.

"The ladies know quality when they see it."

"So do the boys."

"Ain't that the truth!" replied Roscoe slipping into his southern drawl.

Cora Andrews entered the room. Roscoe and I rose from our seats. She looked much younger than she had on our first visit. She was dressed in what looked like an expensive frock.

"Please have a seat. How can I help?" she said as we took our seats. "Would you like some coffee or tea?"

"Coffee for both of us," I said. She reached behind her chair and pulled the bell cord. The maid appeared with a silver service of tea and coffee.

The maid poured out the coffee, and I noticed that she "accidentally" brushed up against Roscoe several times. I gave him a wink.

"That will be all, Maggie," said Mrs. Andrews. The maid nodded and left the room.

"I understand that Mark Johnson was your husband's cousin."

"Yes, that's correct. Such a tragedy to die in the fire."

"Were they close?" I asked.

"Hardly," she replied. "Mark was always asking Dan for money."

"Mark wasn't well off? He had a good job."

"Mark always lived beyond his means, and I suspect that he gambled."

"Suspect?"

"Dan said he suspected Mark gambled."

"I see. When was the last time you saw your husband?"

"The day Mark was killed in the fire. He was going to the office and then he said he had to go away overnight on business to New York."

"Do you know where in New York?"

"I don't know where he was going for business. But he was staying at the Waldorf Astoria."

"Did he check in?"

"Oh, yes. I called there when he didn't come home, and they said he had been there, but had checked out."

"What do you think happened to him?"

"When I saw that the money was missing, I suspected that he was going to invest in a business. I think he was robbed and probably hurt and in a hospital somewhere."

"Did he often carry large amounts of money?"

"On occasion. He was good at investments. That's why he is so successful in business. You just have to find him."

"You don't believe that he took the money and disappeared with the intention of starting a new life?"

"Never!"

"If I may ask, what was the state of your marriage?"

"Dan is devoted to me and the children. He would never abandon his family."

"How many children do you have?"

"Two boys, twelve and fourteen. They are away at school just now."

"Have you told them their father is missing?"

"Not yet. That's why you have to find him."

"I'll do my best. Do you have that picture of your husband?" She got up and went over to the writing desk in the corner, picked up the picture and handed it to me. A sudden thought struck me. "Do you have a photograph of Mark?"

"I think so." She left the room and returned with a photograph. "This is one of Mark and Dan together. It was taken last summer.

"They look remarkably alike," I said as I looked at the picture.

"Yes," she agreed. "They could pass for brothers."

"You're going to New York? In the hot summer?" Velda was incredulous. She put her coffee cup down. "Have you taken leave of your senses?" We were sitting once again in the Dance Department Store restaurant.

"It's work. I'm investigating a missing person. Then I'm off to Philadelphia to check out Ina Patterson's background."

"You lead a very interesting life, Jeremy."

"When are you going to Maine to set up your studio?"

"The sale just went through so I'll be going up tomorrow. Will you come to visit?"

"Of course."

"And bring Rob with you."

"And Tommy Beckford? Will he be there?" Tommy was Velda's love interest of the moment.

"I think I need some time away from Tommy."

"Trouble in paradise?"

"Not really. Tommy is very sweet. But I feel stifled. I need to focus on my painting."

"You're not getting any younger," I pointed out.

"You are the exact same age as me. We're twins remember."

"It's different with men."

Velda made a rude hand gesture in response. "So when are you leaving?"

"Tomorrow. I'll catch the train to New York. Roscoe can keep the house going and Rob will be working."

"How long will you be gone?"

"Not long I shouldn't think." I looked at my watch. "I should be getting back."

"Me, too," said Velda. We paid the bill and left a generous tip.

Roscoe met me at the front door. "Miss Wilde is waiting for you. She seems very agitated. I put her in the upstairs study."

"Thank you, Roscoe. Could you have Jimmy send up a tea tray, please?"

"Certainly."

"Have a seat Miss Wilde," I indicated the red chair by my desk as I took my seat. "What can I do for you?"

"My father is going to marry Ina."

"Yes, so you said before."

"No, I mean they've set a date. They're going to be married next month. You need to prevent it."

"I'm not sure I can prevent it Miss Wilde. The only thing I can do is look into the deaths of her former husbands. And it's just possible that they all died of natural causes."

"But you've got to do something."

"I'm going to Philadelphia shortly, and I'm going to look into her past. That's all I can do at this point. If I find anything out I'll let you know.

But it's entirely possible that your father won't change his plans even if I do."

"I know," she sighed, "but I have to try."

"Trust me Nora. My father married a woman I can't abide so I sympathize with you completely."

Jimmy Kirk came into the study with the tea and coffee service and set it down on the desk.

"Tea or coffee?" I asked.

"Tea please."

I slipped silently beside Judy Hogarth, took a ladle and began doling out soup to the men and women who lined up in the parish hall.

"Jeanine Morrison tells me you've been coming in everyday, Judy."

"Oh, Jeremy. These poor people. It's the least I can do. After all at the end of the day I can slip home to Beacon Hill and have a nice meal. For some of these people this is the only meal of the day."

"I knew there was a heart somewhere in the socialite soul of yours."

"Did you see father Morrison when you came in? He wants to talk to you."

"No, I didn't see him. Do you know what he wanted?" I asked.

"No, but here he comes now."

"Jeremy, just the person I wanted to see. Please come into my office."

James Morrison led me down a hallway where photographic portraits of all the previous rectors looked down from the wall. They were not happy faces. His office was a small room with books piled high on bookcases that seemed to take over the room.

"What can I do for you, Jim?"

"Someone is scamming these poor workers out of what little money they have."

"How so?"

A guy who calls himself Jeff Peters says he an employment recruiter. He claims he can find them a job. All they have to do is pay a small fee. So far there are no jobs."

"How small a fee?"

"Five dollars."

"That's a lot of money for men who are out of work. So he's taken their money and hasn't produced any jobs?"

"Not a one. He says he's working on it. These poor people are so desperate that they want to believe him. Now he says he needs another dollar to complete the process."

"What do you want me to do?"

"I want you to look into it. I want you to take the case."

"I'd like to help," I said. "But I have two cases I'm working on at the moment."

"I understand. But I want to hire you."

"You can't afford to hire me. But I will help as much as I can. How many men have been duped?"

"So far twelve."

I took out my checkbook and wrote a check for sixty dollars and passed it to Jim. "I want you to contact the workers who paid out the five dollars. I want you to tell them that it's a scam and that their money has been refunded. I don't want you to tell anyone that I paid them. But wait until next week to do it. I don't want to tip this guy off that we are on to him. In the mean time I'll take care of Mr. Peters. Do you happen to know where I can find him?"

"No. He just turns up every few days."

"Well, I'll do my best."

"Thank you, Jeremy. You're in my prayers."

"You might want to spend your prayer time on a better cause," I said as we shook hands.

"Not a chance," replied Father Morrison.

Chapter 6

The Windsor Club was almost empty when Rob and I sat down for lunch. He had just finished an early shift. We ordered martinis and the new waiter almost stumbled over himself to be of service.

"What was that all about?" I asked Rob as the waiter went to fetch us the menus.

"Roy is a former rent boy. I ran into him when I was working vice. Being a waiter is a step up for him, and I believe he wants to stay off the streets."

Roy brought us our menus and hovered over us like a mother hen. We both ordered the pot roast special.

"Very good Mr. Dance. Thank you Lieutenant Williams," said Roy as he skipped off to the kitchen.

"Very polite and efficient. Maybe if he doesn't work out here, I could find a job for him at the house," I remarked.

"You could do worse, I'm sure."

"I have a case for you," I said and I outlined for him the scam that Jeff Peters was running in Father Morrison's parish.

"It's unlikely that we can get any of the men to testify against him. They'll be embarrassed that they were scammed. So we need to catch him in the act."

Roy brought our dinners and hovered over us until we sent him away. "Do you know where this guy hangs out?"

"No. Father Morrison says he simply appears every few days," I answered.

"He may not be working alone. He may be part of a bigger scam operation."

"So what do you suggest?"

"Here's what we are going to do," said Rob as he outlined his plan.

"You think the police want to get involved?"

"Oh, yes. It will make a great news story."

"I hope we can wrap it up soon," I sighed. "I have two other cases I need to work on."

"Hopefully it will only take a day or two."

"Can I do anything else for you?" asked Roy as he came to the table to check on us.

"I have a few ideas," I said.

"Jeremy what the hell are you doing and why are you dressed like that?" asked Judy in a shocked voice.

"I'm undercover," I said as I stood in line with the workers and held out my soup bowl to be filled. I had dressed in old clothes as part of my ruse.

"I almost didn't recognize you."

"We'll talk later," I said as I took my bowl of soup and piece of bread and sat down at one of the tables.

"I've never seen you here before," said one of the men. He was taller and more rugged that the others.

"I just lost my job," I said and started to eat. "I don't suppose any of you know where I can get a job?"

Everyone looked at each other and then the tall one said, "There's a guy who comes around who says he can find us jobs. All we have to do is pay five dollars for his expenses."

"That's a lot of money," I remarked.

"I've been out of work for eight months. If I can get a job, then it's worth it."

"Has he gotten anyone a job yet?" I asked.

"Not yet, but he says he knows this construction company that just landed a building contract and there'll be lots of work for everyone."

"Where can I find this guy?"

"He should be checking in tomorrow afternoon," said the tall guy. "My name's Dave."

"Mine's Bruce," I answered with the first name that came to mind. The other men introduced themselves and we shook hands all around. I was in!

It was early evening and I was listening to the radio. The news out of Europe wasn't encouraging, and I was glad Velda had left Germany when she did.

"Telegram for you Mr. Jeremy." Roscoe passed me the wire and waited expectantly. I unfolded the piece of paper and read the contents.

"I wired one of my contacts in New York and had her check at the Waldorf for the missing Dan

Andrews. He was there and the desk clerk confirmed the description. Apparently he checked out yesterday."

"I'm sure he didn't leave a forwarding address," remarked Roscoe.

"Indeed he did not. However, the desk clerk heard him talking to someone on the house phone and he overheard him say something about Niagara Falls."

"You think he's going to go to Canada?"

"That's possible, I suppose."

"What's possible?" asked Rob as he came into the study yawning. He had just woken up from a nap.

I filled him in on the news from the telegraph.

"Who's your contact?"

"Jenny Johnson. She's a detective in her sixties. She can play the little old lady and get all types of information playing the grandmother."

"So are we going to Niagara?"

"If you can spare the time, yes. That's if I can wrap up the scam operation."

"Hopefully you'll be meeting him tomorrow and we'll get a police tail on him. What's happening in the world?"

"The Italians have just invaded Ethiopia. The Germans are getting ready for the Olympic Games. Europe seems to be seething underneath its placid façade."

"I hope we aren't headed into another war," said Rob settling back into the chair.

"I think we've all had enough of war. I sure everyone wants peace. Shall I mix us some cocktails before dinner?"

"That," said Rob, "would be wonderful."

At noon the next day I stood with the men and women waiting in the bread line. Judy doled out a bowl of soup for me and Father Morrison passed me a chunk of bread. Neither of them looked at me as I collected my lunch, but I knew each of them was aware of my presence. Looking around I saw my friends from yesterday at the middle table and I sat down and joined them.

The men nodded at me to acknowledge my presence but kept on eating. Surprisingly the soup was quite tasty and the bread was fresh. I felt sick in the pit of my stomach to know that this was going to be the only meal for some of these folks. The most heart breaking sight of all was to see the mothers with their children. I was determined to hunt down the crooks who preyed on these poor people.

"Is the job guy coming today?" I finally asked.

"He's going to meet us by the old candy factory." The factory was the largest building in the neighborhood. It had been abandoned for three years ever since the company closed its doors. The factory had provided jobs for almost everyone in this neighborhood. Now the building was nothing but a heap of bricks with all the windows broken and boarded up.

"I hope he has good news," said one of the men. The flicker of hope in his eyes was almost too much to stand. I wondered briefly if the Dance Department Store was hiring. I'd have to check it out.

"I scraped together five dollars," I said. "I hope he can find something for me."

"What is it you do?" asked another of the men.

"I'll do almost anything," I said. I saw the looks pass among the men. "What is it?"

"Well, he said it was easier to get places for skilled workers. Laborers are harder to place, so he asks for a few more dollars."

"A few more?" I tried to act surprised.

"It will cost you seven dollars," said the man named Dave.

"But that's all the money I have in the world," I protested. "Can he really find jobs?"

"Yes, he brought one of the guys from his last recruitment. He told us all about how everyone got jobs."

"I see," I said. I was beginning to see very clearly. Hope is a wonderful thing, but it seemed to be clouding these men's vision and making them gullible victims.

We finished eating and took our dirty soup bowls to the service window pass-through to the church kitchen. The kindly volunteers took our bowls and placed them in hot soapy water. I followed the group of men as we headed toward the old candy factory.

"I used to work here," remarked one of the men. He was clearly the oldest of the group and looked pretty much used up. His workers' pants had been mended and his shoes were falling apart.

"What did you used to do?" I asked.

"I was the line foreman. It was a great job. The pay was good and the men and women worked hard."

"What happened to the factory?" I asked.

"One of the big candy companies bought it and then closed it down. Put seventy workers out on the street."

"On the street? What happened to your homes?" I was realizing how out of touch I was.

"Gone," was the answer I got.

"There he is now," said Dave, the leader.

I looked in the direction they were all looking and saw a man of about fifty. He was dressed in a pin stripe suit and was sporting a gold watch chain. His dress gave the appearance of prosperity. The large fedora on his head kept his facial features in the shadows. With him was another man dressed as a worker, but sporting clean clothes and again giving the impression of being well off. No doubt this was another "worker" brought to testify to Peters' success at finding jobs for the unemployed.

"I see you've brought me a new client," said Jeff Peters as he shook my hand.

"I'm Bruce Boyce," I said.

"What type of work are you in Bruce?"

"I'll do anything," I said. "I've been out of work for a long time."

"Then I can help you," stated Peters. "I do ask for a finder's fee, though. It does cost me to make all the contacts."

"Can you really find us jobs?" I asked. I tried to sound desperate.

"Just ask Bobby here," said Peters pointing to the man he had brought along.

"I'm a bricklayer. I'd been out of work for over a year. Jeff here found me a job in three weeks. Now I'm making more money that I've ever made in my life."

I quickly looked at his hands. The man had soft hands and it was clear he had never even picked up a brick let alone worked as a bricklayer. "That's great," I said trying to put on my most hopeful look.

"For a worker like you,' said Peters, "the fee is seven dollars."

"That's an awful lot of money," I said trying to look crestfallen.

"You'll double it in the first week," Peters replied.

I took out my old and battered wallet and carefully counted out seven one dollar bills.

"You're doing the right thing," said Peters. "And now gentlemen," he continued addressing the whole group. "I've been working on your behalf and I've got some new leads. By next week I'll have jobs for all of you."

I knew that by next week Jeff Peters would be long gone along with the money he extorted from the unemployed. Standing on a corner pretending to read a newspaper was a plain clothes policeman watching the whole proceedings.

Chapter 7

Rob was due back at the house for dinner. I was hoping he would have an update for me on Jeff Peters. I needed to get working on the two cases that I was being paid for, but I wanted to make sure that this guy wouldn't be defrauding any more workers.

I heard the front door open and voices as Rob and Roscoe exchanged greetings in the hall. Rob came into the parlor and sat down in his usual seat.

"Did you track down this Peters crook?" I asked.

"Detective O'Malley followed him to a rooming house out on Jamaica Plain. We're keeping an eye on him for a few days to see if he'll lead us to anyone else. We think he's part of a crime gang. We also want to see if he is running the scam on any other workers."

"I really want this guy off the streets. I can't stand the thought that he's preying on the poorest people out there."

"I could arrange for you to come with us."

"I'd like that," I replied. Roscoe came into the room with a cocktail shaker and two glasses.

"You're a gem, Roscoe," said Rob. "I hope you're well paid."

"No complaints, Mr. Rob. Never a dull moment in this house."

We were halfway through dinner when Roscoe came into the dining room and informed Rob that he had a phone call. It was police headquarters.

"It seems that Jeff Peters has a visitor at his rooming house. I've got some men keeping an eye on Peters, but I thought I'd follow his visitor and see what he's up to."

"I'm coming, too," I said.

"Then let's get moving before he disappears."

Roscoe drove us out to Jamaica Plain and dropped us off. The rooming house was a large brick building that had once been a single family home, but now had been broken up to make a rather seedy rooming house.

We located detective O'Malley standing in the shadow of a large elm tree.

"You're still here," said Rob.

"I'm going off duty in about a half hour. Benson is my replacement for the night."

"Is the visitor still there?" I asked.

"As far as I know. He hasn't left, at least not by the front door."

"What's he look like?" asked Rob. "You're the only one who has seen him."

"He's short and very fat. You can't miss him," replied O'Malley.

"Well let's stake out the area and wait for this guy to leave and then follow him," said Rob.

"Roscoe's parked around the corner," I said. "I'll have him move the car, and we can sit and watch the house. No one will think that my car is a police car."

"Good idea," agreed O'Malley.

I found Roscoe around the corner and hopped in the back of the car and quickly told him the plan.

"Nope, never a dull moment," said Roscoe shaking his head.

Rob sat up front with Roscoe and I sat in back with O'Malley. "It could be a long night," warned Rob.

"Be right back," said Roscoe. He got out of the car and disappeared around the corner. Five minutes later he reappeared with four cardboard cups of coffee and a bag of donuts.

"We could use a boy like you at the station," said O'Malley as he bit into a donut.

"Got my hands full working for Mr. Jeremy here," replied Roscoe. I noticed that Roscoe had slipped into a southern drawl. I hate it when someone calls Roscoe a boy. I was just about to set O'Malley straight when the fat man came out of the rooming house.

"There he is," said Rob. "O'Malley, you cover us from that tree over there and wait for your replacement. We need to keep an eye on Peters. Mr. Dance and I will follow the fat man."

"Very good," said O'Malley and stepped out of the car.

"Boy indeed," sniffed Roscoe. I reached over the seat and patted him on the back.

"We'll follow him on foot," said Rob. Roscoe, if you can follow us at a safe distance, do so. But don't worry if you lose us. Just drive home. We'll call you if we need a ride."

"Going to cost you extra," laughed Roscoe as we got out of the car.

"We're too dressed up to be chasing a criminal aren't we?" I asked.

"Actually this is perfect. We look like a couple of swells out on the town. Let's move to the other side of the street and hang back a little."

We crossed the street and let the fat man move ahead about a half block. Several blocks later we saw him enter what appeared to be another rundown rooming house.

"Is he visiting or does he live there?" I asked.

"I'm not sure. We'll have to see if he stays or not."

"That could take hours," I observed.

"Look there," said Rob pointing to an upstairs window. A light had come on and we saw the fat man in the window take off his hat and loosen his tie. He walked away from the window and after a few minutes the lights went out. We waited around for another half hour, but when he didn't reappear we surmised that he lived there.

"Now what?" I asked.

"I'll have a man stake the place out and when he leaves tomorrow we'll have a little talk with the landlady." Rob looked around and spotted a police box. We walked over to it. Rob unlocked it and called headquarters. When he finished he turned to me. "All taken care of. Let's go home and get some sleep."

"That," I said, "is a great idea."

Early the next morning we had a quick breakfast and headed out to Jamaica Plain to the residence of the fat man. We both recognized the plain clothes officer as Dennis Reagan. Dennis, like Rob, was from a wealthy family and like Rob he liked the excitement of police work.

"Dennis," I greeted him, "How did you end up on this assignment?"

"I saw that Williams here was on the case and figured I'd better give him a hand. What are you doing here? Last time I checked you weren't on the force."

"I'm working on a case which is connected to this one." I went on to explain my involvement.

"At least you get to pick and choose your cases."

"While you two were socializing," said Rob, "the fat man left the house." Dennis and I looked around to see the fat man disappear around the corner. "Time to have a talk with the land lady."

We walked up the steps and rang the door bell. A plump sixty-something woman dressed in black answered the door. Dennis and Ron showed their police shields. I flipped open my private investigator badge and hoped she didn't look too closely at it.

"I run a respectable house," she said with a frown.

"We just have a few questions for you," said Rob. She motioned us into a small front parlor. The furnishings were in good condition and rather ornate. The inside of the house was in much better condition than the outside appeared.

"What do you want?" she said without a smile.

"Were investigating one of your boarders," replied Dennis.

"All the gentlemen of this house are respectable working men."

"I'm sure that's true," I said taking over the conversation. "This is obviously a quality residence."

"I'm glad you can see that," she said and relaxed. "I'm Anna Miller. When my husband died I had to take in boarders to make ends meet."

"I can tell you're a good business woman." Finally she smiled at me, though she gave the other two a less than friendly look. "We just need some information about one of your boarders. We believe he might be involved in a crime, and I'm sure as a respectable business woman you'd like to help."

"Of course, Mr...?"

"Dance," I answered and smiled. Dennis and Rob were looking at me with new respect. Flattery opens more doors than the tough police approach I always feel.

"I can't believe one of my boarders is a criminal."

"He may not be. We're just trying to eliminate him as a suspect."

"Oh, I see. Which gentleman is it?"

"We don't have a name. We were hoping you could tell us. He's a rather large gentleman."

"Oh, that would be Mr. Crosby."

"What can you tell us about him, Mrs. Miller?" I shot Dennis and Rob a look to keep them quiet.

"Charles Crosby. He's a business man."

"What type of business?" asked Rob. Mrs. Miller gave him a dirty look and turned to me.

"He said he's an investor of some kind."

"Do you know where he works?" asked Dennis.

"He's office is downtown. At least that's what he says."

"Do you know where downtown?" I asked.

"I don't believe he ever said. I don't like to pry."

"Of course not," I agreed. "Does he keep regular hours?"

"He leaves most mornings and comes back in the afternoon. Nice hours if you ask me."

"Does he go out in the evening?" I asked.

"Maybe two or three times a week," she said after a slight pause.

"Do you think we could have a look at his room?" asked Rob.

"Oh, I don't know about that," she said looking puzzled.

"It might help clear him," I said. "I'm sure you wouldn't want any trouble. If it got around that one of your guests was a criminal…"

"I guess it would be okay," she answered quickly. We followed her upstairs and down the hall past four or five closed doors. She took us into a rather large room with a double bed, a dresser, and a small sitting area with a sofa and chair and a small bookcase.

We looked around but didn't see anything out of the ordinary. Rob checked the dresser and Dennis checked the closet. I had learned from previous cases that books make good hiding places. I went to the bookcase and started looking through the books. It only took me a few minutes before I found something.

"Hey, take a look at this," I said. I passed them a book that had been carefully hollowed out. In the book was a large pile of bills.

"That's a lot of money," remarked Mrs. Miller.

"It is indeed," I said as I counted out two thousand dollars.

Mindful that I had two other cases to work on, I was becoming impatient with the progress on this case. It was time to wrap it up. I could just walk away and leave the case to the police, but Father Morrison had asked me to help and I was determined to see it through.

"I don't understand." Mrs. Miller looked very unhappy. "Maybe he doesn't trust banks."

"It's not likely that a man whose business is in finance would be distrustful of banks," I said.

"We think," added Rob, "that he is the head of a gang that is taking money from the unemployed, promising them jobs, and then disappearing with the money."

"That son of a bitch," snapped Mrs. Miller and then covered her mouth in embarrassment.

"Hey guys, over here," said Dennis Reagan. He was busy going through the pockets of a suit coat hanging in the closet. "I've found a piece of paper with three addresses on it. One of the addresses belongs to Jeff Peters."

"That's the guy who's hanging out at St. Martin's." I said. "We can assume that the other two are working the same type of scam in other parts of the city."

"Time we paid a little visit to Mr. Peters," added Rob. "Hopefully we can get him to squeal on this Crosby guy."

"I'll have some men round up the guys at the other two addresses," said Dennis.

Now we were getting somewhere.

Chapter 8

Jeff Peters wasn't at home when Rob and I called. "We'll wait," Rob told the landlady. She was in her early thirties and very pretty. Not at all what I pictured a landlady should look like.

"Suit yourselves," she told us. "I have things to do."

"Friendly sort," I remarked after she left.

"She doesn't like cops. I'm sure she's had a run-in or two."

"What type of run-in would a landlady have?"

"The boarding house is just a front. I'll bet some of her boarders are ladies of the evening."

"Really?" Just then I caught sight of Jeff Peters coming up the walkway. He looked surprised to see me and it showed on his face, but he quickly recovered. He then seemed to recognize me.

"Bruce, isn't it?"

"Yes, sir."

"I'm still working on finding you a job. I should have some information for you in a few days."

"That won't be necessary," said Rob flashing his police badge at Peters. The color seemed to drain out of Peter's face.

"I see how it is," replied Peters reaching into his pocket and pulling out a roll of bills. "How much?"

"I'd say about ten to twenty in the big house," I said.

"I'm sure we can reach a deal," Peters pulled out another roll of bills from another pocket.

"Here's the deal," said Rob. "You help us bring down your boss Crosby and you might get a reduced sentence."

"Okay, okay. I know when to cut my losses." Peters sang like a birdie and told us all we needed to put Crosby away. Rob was busy writing notes. I had to ask Peters to slow down a bit so Rob could get his notes organized. Finally Rob had all the information he needed.

"I suggest you let Mr. Dance here return all the money back to the workers you swindled. It might help your case when it comes to trial."

"Fine," said Peters and tossed me his roll of bills. Two uniformed officers led Peters away.

I turned to Rob, "Are you in any way authorized to offer a deal?"

"Not that I know of," he said and smiled. "I did say 'might help' didn't I?"

"Yes, you did."

"The good news," I said to Father Morrison, "is that Peters kept good records. It should be easy to return the money to the right persons." I passed him the roll of bills and the notes I had taken from Peters' room.

"I can't thank you enough, Jeremy. What cases are you working on next?"

"I've got two I need to get moving on."

"Best of luck, Jeremy. I hope to see you here some Sunday."

"You never know, father. You never know."

"Will there be anything else, Mr. Dance?" asked Jimmy Kirk as he placed the drinks tray on the parlor table.

"No, thank you, Jimmy. You're free to go. And if I'm not mistaken there's a young man downstairs waiting for you."

"Yes, sir," he said and laughed.

"You really lucked out with Jimmy and Roscoe," said Rob as he passed me a cocktail.

"You live here too," I replied. "At least most of the time. Why you keep that Brookline apartment is beyond me."

"I'm not sure the police department would approve of my living with a private detective in a Beacon Hill mansion. They might get ideas."

"I've got some ideas."

"So have I," he said and looked at me with a look I'd come to know well."

"I'm heading off to New York tomorrow," I said changing the subject.

"Looking for Cora Andrews's missing husband?"

"Yes, I've been delayed too long, and I need to find him before he disappears completely."

"What about the Black Widow case?"

"Ina Patterson? I don't think she's a Black Widow. Old men die. I think Nora Wilde may be just imagining the whole thing. But just in case I'll be looking into Ina's background. There's no rush on that case. She'd have no reason to get rid of Nora's father until after the wedding."

"Where do you find these cases?" asked Rob.

"Actually, they find me. Now drink up. It's time for bed."

To get to Niagara Falls I had to take the train into New York and transfer to Buffalo, and then take a local up to the falls. Stopping in New York gave me the chance to check in with my New York contact Jenny Johnson.

"It seems," said Jenny as we sat in a booth at Jerome's Deli on upper Fifth Avenue, "that Mr. Andrew's wasn't alone."

"Let me guess," I said. "He had a young woman with him."

"She wasn't that young, but yes."

"Do we know who she is?"

"Of course. That's what you pay me to find out," replied Jenny grinning at me. "I'm very good at my job."

"Yes, you are. Now tell me."

"Her name is Viola Flowers. I'm guessing that that is her stage name."

"Stage name? So she's an actress?"

"She does a little song and dance routine for a vaudeville company. It seems they were in Boston last month before coming here."

"Most likely that's how Andrews met her."

"And guess where they're playing now?

"Niagara Falls?"

"Exactly. So it's likely that Andrews is with her."

"Feel like a trip to Niagara Falls?" I asked.

"Sure thing."

On the train we came up with a plan. Jenny was going to play a retired theater performer, and I would play the dutiful son, hoping that we could get in with the vaudeville people. Our story would be that my "mother" was trying to get us both into a show. The first order of business was to find out where the troupe was staying. Most likely it would be a theatrical boarding house.

From experience we knew that train porters and café workers were the best sources for local information.

"Traveling with you, Jeremy is a treat. I don't often get to travel first class." We were having cocktails and lunch in the first class dining car.

"You should charge more for your expenses. You're one of the best detectives I know."

"I hope I can live up to your expectations."

"Good detecting is eighty percent luck."

"That's so true," she said as she tucked into her lunch.

"Excuse me," I said to the dining car waiter. "We're traveling to Niagara Falls. We're private detectives on a case." The waiter's eyes got big as I showed him my license. "I'll bet someone like you has plenty of friends in the area."

"Yes sir."

"We need to connect with someone who knows the area and what goes on there, if you get my drift."

"You go to the Falls View Hotel and have dinner in the dining room. The head waiter is Jimmy Brown. You talk to him. He knows who's coming and going in town."

"Thank you." I passed him a five dollar bill.

"Yes sir." He gave a bow and left us.

At Buffalo's Central Station we changed trains to Niagara. It was too late in the day to really do anything once we arrived so we checked into the Falls View Hotel.

The hotel lobby was busy as I made my way to the front desk and booked two rooms for the night. Despite the belief that Niagara Falls was a honeymoon destination, I didn't see any evidence of newlyweds as I looked around. Mostly I saw elderly men and women, foreign tourists, and businessmen.

"Will you be staying long?" asked the desk clerk.

"At least for one night, maybe longer."

"Very good, sir. I've given you two rooms on the top floor with a view of the falls. I hope you enjoy your stay. I'll have the bellboy take up your bags."

"Very kind of you," I said and passed him a tip. "Any help would be appreciated."

"You have but to ask." Jenny joined me at the front desk, and I passed her the keys.

Jenny's room was several doors down from mine. We agreed to meet in the hotel bar room at six o'clock. The room was on the small side, but had a sitting area, private bath, and as promised, a view of the falls.

There was a knock at the door and the bellboy brought in my bag. "Anything else I can do for you sir?" He looked me up and down, and I recognized the look.

"When do you get off work?"

"Ten tonight. I could stop by and see if you need anything."

"Stop by if you'd like."

"I'd like that very much," he said smiling.

"A very handsome uniform," I said. He was dressed in a red uniform with gold braid and a red hat.

"You should see me out of uniform."

"That is a very good idea," I said.

"My room is very nice," said Jenny as we sipped cocktails in the hotel bar.

"I figured we could use a little luxury before we go to a boarding house."

"If we can find the boarding house."

"Hopefully the tip we got about the head waiter will pan out." I pulled out my pocket watch and looked at the time. "Ready for dinner?"

"Absolutely.

Chapter 9

T he hotel dining room was larger than needed for a small hotel. It was obvious that it served as many visitors as hotel guests. Crystal chandeliers, candlelight, and white linen tablecloths made a more formal setting than I expected.

"Table for two," I said to the head waiter.

"Right this way," he said as he led us to a table in the corner.

"Are you Jimmy Brown by any chance?" I asked.

"Yes, I am."

"Would you stop by our table when we've finished eating?" asked Jenny.

"Certainly."

The menu was extensive, and we both order the rainbow trout with roasted potatoes and minted peas. They had a good wine selection and we managed to finish off a bottle of 1924 French white with no difficulty. When we finished eating the head waiter came over.

"What can I do for you?" he asked.

"The porter on the train," I began, "gave your name as being someone in the know about the goings on in town."

"I pride myself on being informed," he said and smiled.

I explained that we were detectives, and that we were looking for a vaudeville troupe who had just arrived in town and where they might be staying.

"They would be staying at the River House down on Water Street. That's where all the theater people stay. It's more boarding house than hotel, but I understand it's quite nice for what it is."

"Thank you," I said as I passed him a generous tip. He smiled and bowed.

"I think," said Jenny, "that we're in for an adventure in lodging."

The River House was an old, rambling structure that had once been a first class hotel, but now was in a less fashionable part of town. Above the front door were placed the comedy and tragedy masks that identified it as a specialty hotel.

Jenny and I checked out of the Falls View Hotel and spent the afternoon sightseeing along the falls. We even took a ride of the Maid of the Mist. The boat took us right up to the falls. Later we collected our luggage and presented ourselves at the River House. As it happened they had rooms available. The rooms were clean, but not as luxurious as the rooms at the Falls View Hotel.

By the time I made my way to the lobby, Jenny was already ensconced with the residents. "Here's my son Jeremy Smith. He's a gifted piano player. Jeremy, this is Mr. Hammond. He's the head of the acting troupe. I'm sorry, I didn't get the name of the company."

"Hammond Players," he said and shook my hand. "I understand that you and your mother have an act you're trying to get staged."

"That's right," I said. I had no idea what Jenny had got us in to.

"Yes," said Jenny quickly. "Jeremy accompanies me on the piano. I was a fairly good soprano in my time. After poor Jeremy's father died I had to go on the road to support us."

"I'd love to hear you. Maybe you'd play for us later. Now if you'll excuse me I have to round up my players for dinner."

"What the hell," I said to Jenny.

"You do play the piano don't you?"

"Yes, but hardly concert worthy."

"Not to worry," she said waving her hand. "I can sing a fair bit if I do say so. And we're not actually looking for a job."

"No. but we need to be credible."

"You worry too much." Jenny seemed to be enjoying herself. "Come over and meet Mary Marguerite Burke." She led me over to a young blonde girl in curls. From a distance she looked like a ten year old, but as I got closer I could see that she was well into her twenties. "Mary Marguerite, this is my son Jeremy."

"Pleased to meet you Jeremy." She looked me up and down and smiled, apparently liking what she was seeing. It's about time we got some young blood here."Most of the men in theater are either too old or, you know," she flicked her wrist making a limp motion.

"Isn't that the truth," agreed Jenny. I gave her the evil eye, but she just ignored me. "Mary Marguerite is a ventriloquist."

"And a very beautiful one at that," I said hoping that flattery would get me some mileage. It worked as she rewarded me with a smile.

"Maybe you and I can go for a walk later," she said to me.

"I'd be honored," I replied.

"Well, I've got to go freshen up before dinner," she said as she hurried off.

"Nicely played," Jenny said to me.

One of the characteristics of a theatrical hotel or boarding house is the meal schedule. Supper was served at five in order to get the actors off to the theater for the evening performance. I wasn't used to eating that early, but supper gave me a chance to scope out the rest of the residents. I was looking for Viola Flowers, but I learned that she was dining out this evening.

"What is Miss Flowers' act?" I asked Jimmy Hammond who was seated next to me at one of the large tables.

"Viola is a dancer. She and her sister do a number at the beginning of the act." I learned that the show consisted of a comedian who warmed up the audience, a string quartet, the Flowers sister's dance number, Mary Marguerite Burke's ventriloquist act, and then a feature film. These days vaudeville acts tended to be opening acts for motion pictures.

Iris Flowers and her sister Viola were, I learned to my dismay, twins. It was going to be harder to keep an eye on Viola if she looked like her sister. After dinner Jenny and I introduced ourselves to Iris.

"Are you coming to the theater tonight?" she asked.

"We wouldn't miss it, would we Jeremy?" said Jenny using a very motherly tone.

"Are you looking for a place in the show?" asked Iris giving us the once over.

"Maybe sometime," answered Jenny. "We're really out of practice."

"Well. I'm sure you'll fit right in."

Just then Mary Marguerite Burke came over and joined us. "How about that walk, Jeremy?" she said giving Iris a withering look. "I've got about a half hour before I have to get to the theater."

"My pleasure," I said as she took my arm.

"Have you seen the falls? They're quite impressive."

"Only briefly."

"Well there's a great view of the falls from the end of this street. Are you looking to join the company? We could use a nice looking young man."

"My mother is the talent. I'm just the key pounder."

"I'm sure you're too modest."

"I'm looking forward to the show tonight," I said to change the subject. "I can't wait to see your act." Actually I'm not at all fond of ventriloquist acts. I appreciate the talent, but if you've seen one wise cracking dummy, you've seen them all.

"It's just one of my many talents." I pretty much could guess what her other talents were and thought I better change the subject fast.

"What's the Flowers sisters' act like?" I asked.

"Those two tramps? They just clunk along on stage. They call it tap dancing, but it looks more like stomping on bugs if you ask me."

"I didn't see the other sister at dinner," I said hoping she could add some information. By now we were at the end of the street. Ahead of us was the falls. You could actually hear the roar and see the mist rising up from the falls.

"She's taken up with some new guy. He's some sleaze ball she met in New York, I think." There was some emotion in her eyes I couldn't read. "He flashes his money around. Why all this interest?"

"I like to know about people, especially if I'm going to be around them."

"Viola has also been stringing Hammond along, kissing up to the manager so she and her sister can get more stage time. She's nothing but a whore."

"I should probably get you back to the hotel so you can get to the theater," I said before she went off on a rant.

"Yes, I suppose," she answered.

"Well?" asked Jenney when I returned to the hotel. "What did you learn?"

"Not much," I answered. "Other than that there's no love lost between Miss Burke and the Misses Flowers. And it seems that Viola has taken on a new boyfriend who seems to have some money."

"Do you think this boyfriend is the missing Andrews?"

"It all seems to fit. We should be able to find out pretty soon. We need to wrap this up."

"You have another case lined up?"

"Yes, as a matter of fact." I told her about Ina Patterson.

"Do you have an operative in Philadelphia?"

"No. Even though it's my home town and I have no desire to go back. I think I'll send Roscoe ahead and see what he can dig up."

"Probably a good idea. It'll save you some leg work, and we operatives need the work."

"What do you say we go to the theater and see a show?"

"I think that's a good idea."

"We can stop at the telegraph office on the way. I'll send a wire off to Roscoe."

Chapter 10

The Niagara Opera House was a small venue of about one hundred and fifty seats. I was surprised to find it almost full as Jenney and I were shown to our seat by the uniformed usher. The play bill was much as Jimmy Hammond had described. The featured film was called *The Bohemian Girl* and starred Oliver and Hardy with Thelma Todd.

"How bad do you think this show is going to be?" asked Jenny.

"Vaudeville is in for a rough time, I fear. Most people probably just want to see the film."

The lights dimmed and the band began tuning up and shortly after played a warm-up number. The comedian, George Penny according to the program, came out on stage. He was wearing his jacket wrong-side out, his tie was twice as long as normal, his straw hat had no top and his shoes were enormous. The audience began laughing before he even opened his mouth. I found the jokes to be tired and corny, but it seemed that the audience didn't share my views as they laughed at all of his jokes.

The string quartet was up and they played chamber music. I recognized the piece as Haydn's "The Lark." They were really quite talented, and I wondered why they were relegated to playing in a second rate vaudeville troupe.

There was a brief intermission and then the Flowers sisters were on stage. I had to admit that as

77

tap dancers go, the sisters were pretty good. Their costumes were a bright red and the cut of the dress accentuated their legs, which even I had to admit were attractive. They seemed to dance in perfect rhythm to the music. They received a standing ovation at the end of their act.

Mary Marguerite Burke's ventriloquist act followed the Flowers sisters. She came out on stage dressed as a little girl wearing a white apron. The dummy was a very large teddy bear and the chair she sat in was oversized giving the illusion that she was tiny. She bantered with the dummy, and she was really quite good, but the audience was getting restless. At the end of her act there was polite applause, but nothing like the reception of the Flowers sisters.

"No wonder she hates the Flowers sisters," whispered Jenny.

"Her act isn't bad, but it's poorly placed in the show," I whispered back. After all the acts came out to take a bow, there was another intermission and then the movie started. All in all, the movie was the best part of the show. I'm sure the rest of the audience felt the same way.

"There's a telegram for you Mr. Smith," said the desk clerk when we returned to the hotel. It took me a minute to figure out that he was talking to me. Jenny had registered us as the Smith mother and son team.

"Thank you," I said as I took the telegram.

"Well," said Jenny, "I think I'll call it a night. You had better too, before the theater ladies return and try to ravish you. Unless you'd like to try out that side of the fence."

"Thanks. I think I'll take your advice." I returned to my room and read the telegram. Roscoe's telegram confirmed that he got my message and was on his way to Philadelphia. Ina Patterson's first marriage had ended with the death of her husband. I knew Roscoe could find out if there was anything unusual about the death. I'd try to join him as soon as I finished up here. All I had to do was track down Viola Flowers' boy friend, whom I was pretty sure was the missing Daniel Andrews. So far Viola Flowers had eluded me, but I knew she'd be at the hotel at some point.

I slept later than usual and when I went down for breakfast most of the vaudeville troupe was having breakfast. Once again I looked around and didn't see Viola, though her sister was here. I went up to the buffet and took a plate and filled it with eggs, bacon, and toast.

"May I join you?" I asked Iris Flowers who was seated at a small table by herself.

"Of course, Jeremy," she smiled. "I'd love to have some company."

"I loved your act," I said. "I was hoping to meet your sister."

"She's probably not up yet." I gave her a questioning look. I assumed they shared a room.

"She has her own room. Growing up we had to share everything. It's been nice to have a little separation."

"I see," I said.

"You can't imagine what it's like to have a twin. You have to share everything."

"Actually," I said, "I have a twin sister. It's not quite the same, of course, but I understand."

"Do the two of you get along?"

"Oh, yes," I replied. "We're quite the best of friends. I can't imagine my life without her."

"I envy you. Viola and I bicker all the time."

"Well, hello!" said Mary Marguerite Burke as she plunked herself down at the table uninvited. "Hope I'm not interrupting anything."

"We just discovered that we're both twins," said Iris, trying to be friendly.

"Funny you two don't look alike," Mary Marguerite said, laughing at her own joke,

"I was just saying how much I enjoyed the show," I said to change the subject.

"Did you like my act?"

"You're very talented," I said. And a super bitch I thought to myself. The three of us chatted for a little while longer and then I returned to my room to try to figure out my next move.

I was sitting at the desk looking over my notes when I heard pounding and loud voices coming from the hallway. I opened the door to the hall to see what the commotion was.

"Viola, open this door!" It was Iris pounding on what I gathered was Viola's door. "We need to rehearse."

"Maybe she went out," I suggested.

"The desk clerk said she came in early this morning and he hasn't seen her leave."

"What's all he racket?" asked Mary Marguerite Burke as she opened her door and peered out in the hallway.

"Viola won't answer the door," explained Iris.

Mary Marguerite Burke walked down to the end of the hall and pounded on Viola's door. "What's going on? Open up Viola."

"Go away," replied a faint voice from behind the door. "I have a headache."

"Mystery solved," said Mary Marguerite Burke. "Now stop all the racket. Jeremy, how about walking me to the theater?"

"Sure thing," I answered, though the last thing I wanted to do was spend more time with Mary Marguerite Burke. But I figured I might get more information from her.

"Let me grab a sweater and I'll meet you in the lobby."

Jenny was in the lobby sitting at a table playing solitaire. "What's the plan?" she asked as I sat down at the table.

"We need to find Dan Andrews. I'm not having much luck with Iris and Viola's been elusive. There can't be that many places for him to be."

"I expect he'll show up at the hotel at some point."

"Yes, but time is money and the sooner we find him the better for our client."

"Ready Jeremy?" Mary Marguerite Burke was dressed up and had a considerable amount of makeup on.

"Excuse me, mother," I said to Jenny. "I'm walking Mary Marguerite to the theater."

"Well enjoy, son."

"Your mother seems nice," said Mary Marguerite once we were outside.

"Most of the time. Too bad about Viola's headache," I said. "I've been wanting to meet her."

"Why? You've met the sister. If you've seen one you've seen them both."

"I think her boyfriend is an old friend of mine. I lost track of him some time ago. You've met him, right?"

"I've seen him, but I haven't met him." There was something odd about her voice, and I suspected she wasn't being totally truthful.

I pulled out the photograph of Dan Andrews and his cousin Mark. "Is this him?"

She looked at the photograph. "Yes," she said.

"Do you know where he is staying?"

"I think he's at a hotel on the Canadian side of the falls. I overheard Viola say that she was tired of trekking across the border to see him."

"Do you know which hotel?" I asked.

"No," she shook her head. We arrived at the theater a few minutes later. "How about a late supper some night soon?" she asked.

"That would be great," I lied. She smiled and went into the theater.

I needed some time to think, so I walked down the hill to Bridal Veil Falls and sat on the wall and watched the tourists. The roar of the falls was amazing. I thought this would be a good place to visit when I wasn't working. Maybe Rob and I could come here sometime.

When I returned to the hotel there were three police cars out front and the residents were all lined up in the lobby. There was a general air of confusion and chaos and a general buzz of hushed voices.

"What's going on?" I asked Jenny when I found her sitting on a sofa in the corner.

"It's Viola Flowers. She's been murdered!"

Chapter 11

The death of Viola Flowers had been discovered when the maid entered the room to clean. Viola had been found crumpled up on the floor. According to the police she must been hit hard in the head. There was a pool of blood on the floor.

The police began by interviewing everyone at the hotel. The body had been removed and taken to the coroner. The hotel staff was questioned first and then the vaudeville troupe. Jenny and I were the only other guests at the hotel and they saved us for last. Several of the troupe were in tears and an uneasy silence pervaded the lobby.

"Mr. Smith is it?" asked the plainclothes detective. He introduced himself as Glen Fletcher.

"It's Dance actually," I said as I passed him my business card.

"You're working a case, Mr. Dance?"

"I'm looking for a missing person who may have ties to Viola Flowers."

"Really?" That got his attention. "So you made her acquaintance?"

"Actually, I've never met her. She hasn't been around for the last few days, and I've only been here for two days."

"Have you observed anything unusual here?"

"Such as?"

"Any gossip?"

"Not really. I saw the show. She and her sister had a pretty good act. There might have been some professional jealousy among the players, but nothing deadly as far as I could see."

"Are you planning to stick around for a day or two?"

"Yes, I'm still looking for a missing husband."

"If you hear or notice anything would you let us know?"

"Of course. I've worked with the police before."We shook hands and I promised to keep in touch.

Jenny had pretty much the same interview experience as I. It was getting late, and we decided to get lunch in town and get away from the hotel for a while. I suggested we walk across the bridge to the Canadian side of the falls.

Walking away from the falls we found a small Italian restaurant with a distant view of the Canadian falls. The hostess sat us at a table near the window and passed us menus. We both ordered a beer and lasagna.

"How do you think this will affect our search?" Jenny asked me when we had been served our beer.

"Dan Andrews might make an appearance. On the other hand he might be involved."

"You think he could have killed her?"

"No, it had to be someone at the hotel. According to the desk clerk no one from the outside came in and we know the approximate time of death."

"We do?"

"We heard her this morning when she refused to come out of her room. We know the body was discovered around eleven thirty, so she had to have been murdered between ten and eleven this morning."

"Well that really is police business isn't it?"

"True enough, except that we are probably on the suspect list like everyone else."

"I was in the lobby during that time period and the desk clerk can vouch for me," said Jenny.

"And I was walking to the theater with Mary Marguerite, so I think we're in the clear."

"It will be interesting to see who doesn't have an alibi."

"And who had a motive," added Jenny.

Just then our lunch was served.

"While we're here," I said after a few minutes of silence as we ate, "Let's check some of the hotels around here and see if anyone can identify Andrews."

"I guess it wouldn't hurt." We finished lunch with coffee and pastry.

There were several hotels located near the falls.

"If Dan Andrews had arrived in Niagara by train he would have had to walk to the hotel from the station, or taken a cab to the bridge and walked over to Canada. I theorized that his hotel had to be in walking distance to the River House where Viola was staying.

At the first hotel I showed the desk clerk the picture I had brought and asked if he had seen the gentleman.

"Which one?" He asked. I had brought the photograph of Dan Andrews and his cousin.

"The one on the left." He looked carefully at the photo.

"No, sorry. I can tell you for sure that he didn't stay here."

"Thank you for your time," said Jenny as we headed out.

The next hotel we tried was much the same story. The fourth hotel we hit pay dirt.

"That's Mr. Andrews," said the clerk as he looked at the picture. "Who's the other guy? I haven't seen him."

"That's his cousin. Is Mr. Andrews here?"

"No, he left earlier. He usually comes back in the late afternoon."

"Thank you. We'll check back later."

"So he is here then?" said Jenny as we walked back across the river to our hotel.

"Yes he is. But whether he wants to be found and returned to his wife is another matter."

"Just a guess," said Jenny. "But if he's here and has a new girlfriend, I doubt that he wants to return to Boston."

"Well at least we can be done with the case. I have a plan."

We returned to the River House. The lobby, which had seemed so chaotic earlier, had sunk into a quiet gloom. Apparently the show was in some disarray because of the death and was likely to be canceled. So much for the show must go one.

"Just the two I was looking for," said Robert Hammond, the manager of the troupe. He motioned Jenny and me to sit down. "As you know we're down an act because of the recent unpleasantness. Perhaps the two of you could fill in?"

"Excuse me?" I didn't quite understand.

"Your mother wants to get back into show business. This is an opportunity."

"We'd love to," cooed Jenny as she slid her hand over Hammond's.

"But…" I began to protest, but Jenny shot me a warning look.

"It's settled then. I assume you are good?"

"It's been a while," smiled Jenny. "But yes, we're good." Hammond excused himself and went up to his room.

"Are you crazy?" I yelled.

"It'll be fun."

"Fun? They'll boo us off the stage. Besides we know where Andrews is now. We don't need a cover."

"Don't be too hasty, Jeremy. There's been a murder in this hotel and we might be able to help. I've been doing this job as long as you've been alive. Trust me."

"In that case," I sighed. "We had better begin rehearsing."

"And there's a piano over there in the corner. Let's go."

Luckily Jenny had a nice voice, and we were able to cobble together an act that would be passable. At four o'clock we headed back across the border to face Dan Andrews. The desk clerk said he hadn't returned yet so Jenny and I took a seat in the lobby to wait for him.

"Maybe he's run off. Maybe he killed Viola," remarked Jenny.

"He may not even know about it yet. It's only been about six hours."

The lobby door opened we both looked up. A man walked in but it wasn't Dan Andrews.

"It can't be!" I exclaimed.

"You said he died in a fire."

"We thought he did."

The man in the lobby was Dan Andrews's cousin, Mark Johnson.

Chapter 12

Jenny looked at me over her glasses. "I don't understand."

"Let's get out of here before he sees us." We beat a hasty retreat from the hotel lobby and headed back to the River House. "Clearly Mark Johnson didn't die in the fire. It was Johnson that people recognized in the picture, not Andrews. I never gave it a thought."

"Then whose body was in the burned wreckage?" Jenny asked. She thought about it a minute. "It was Dan Andrews wasn't it?"

"That would be my guess. This presents a whole new scenario. This is no longer a missing person's case. This is murder."

"And the financial papers?"

"My guess is that Johnson has them, and they didn't burn in the fire."

"How very clever."

"How very evil."

"Hey, slow down. I'm an old woman." I had begun to pick up my pace as my mind was racing as we walked back to the hotel.

"Sorry," I said.

"So what are we going to do?"

I took out my pocket watch and looked at the time. "We're due at the theater in two hours. There's not much we can do at the moment. Tomorrow we'll go to the police, but if Johnson stays in Canada that's going to make it more complicated."

A fresh crop of tourists had arrived in Niagara and the theater was full. That wasn't doing much for my nerves. After we had rehearsed our act we waited in the wings until our turn came up. The wardrobe mistress had supplied me with a tuxedo that almost fit, and Jenny had a sparkling sequined gown. Both of us had to be pinned into our costumes and hoped that nothing popped off during the performance.

I watched the stage hands move the grand piano out on the stage and then our act was announced. "Ladies and Gentlemen. Straight from New York City is the mother and son team of Smith and Smith." There was light applause as we crossed the stage and took our positions. I sat at the piano and hoped my fingers would remember what to do.

We started out with the popular "Smoke Gets in Your Eyes." Jenny had a great soprano voice, and I managed to pound on the keys correctly. We were both surprised that the audience clapped so enthusiastically. The next song we sang as a duo was "Tumbling Tumbleweeds" as I added my tenor voice to the mix. We were shocked when the audience went wild. Mr. Hammond the manager gave us the high sign and held up a hand written sign that said "Keep Going."

We ended the set with Cole Porter's "Night and Day." We were called out for a second curtain call and Mr. Hammond rushed over to us and gave us a hug. "You've saved the show."

"Really?" I asked. I thought we did a passable job, but neither of us was a professional.

"Really! You've got the job."

I started to protest, but Jenny gave me a kick. "That's great news, Mr. Hammond," she said. "Count us in."

As soon as he was out of ear shot I turned to her. "Are you crazy? We've got to wrap this up."

"We might need the cover for another day or two. Relax." I had the feeling that Jenny was enjoying herself.

It was late when we got back to the hotel. I went up to my room where someone had slipped a telegram under my door. I open it. It was from Roscoe telling me he had arrived in Philadelphia and was checking out the records of Ina Patterson's first husband's death. I doubted he could find out much, but I could be wrong. I was beginning to have an uneasy feeling about Ina Patterson.

At first I had dismissed Nora Wilde's fears as just concern that her father was remarrying, but the more I thought about it the more I considered that she might be right. My father had remarried and his new wife was nothing but a gold digging tramp. Men were fools when it came to women.

My thoughts were interrupted by a knock on the door. I opened it to find Mary Marguerite Burke standing there with a flask in her hand.

"I saw your light on, and I thought you might like a night cap." She was wearing a revealing night gown that was just barely covered over with a see-through robe.

"That's very kind of you," I said thinking fast. "But I was just about to go out. I'm meeting someone for a late supper."

"Well, I won't keep you," she said in a huff and stomped off. Clearly Mary Marguerite wasn't used to being turned down.

I needed to get hold of Rob and tell him about Mark Johnson. This was a case for the Boston police. I didn't want anyone to overhear my phone call, so I grabbed my jacket and went in search of a phone booth.

Rob got on the next train to New York and had arrived in Niagara after a series of transfers. Along with Jenny we were sitting in the Niagara Falls police station and talking with a detective named Ken McKenzie.

"The problem," he said, "is that he's staying in Canada. If we could get him here we could avoid a ton of paperwork and arrest him on suspicion of murder."

"Well," said Rob, "if we can find the financial certificates in his possession, then we can at least arrest him for theft. The murder rap will be all circumstantial, but it might be enough."

"But supposedly no one entered or left the hotel until after the murder. So how could he be guilty?" I asked.

"No one was *seen* entering or leaving," said McKenzie. "There are windows and fire escapes."

"We'll have customs pick him up if he tries to cross the border," added McKenzie. "His girlfriend was murdered, and we need to know where he was at the time. He's a suspect in that case."

"Isn't that enough for the Canadian police to pick him up?" I asked.

"Yes, but if they determine that he has an alibi for that time, then they won't pursue it, and we'll have tipped our hand," McKenzie said as he crushed out his cigarette in the ash tray on his desk.

"Any leads at all in the Flowers's murder?" asked Jenny.

"She was alive in the morning and," he said as he turned to me, "you said you heard her and then everyone at the hotel has an alibi after that. So no one apparently knows anything. And we can't find a motive."

"If there were a man involved," sighed Jenny, "That would explain everything."

Something in my brain clicked, and I had an idea. "Something just occurred to me," I said and then I explained my plan.

"Do you really think it will work?" asked Jenny as the three of us had lunch in a tea room near the falls on the Canadian side.

"If one of them is the murderer, then yes, I think it will work."

"And the motive?" asked Rob.

"Jealousy, both personal and professional."

"Let's give it a whirl," said Jenny.

Chapter 13

Rob was staying at the Falls View Hotel since Jenny and I were still undercover. I skipped the meager breakfast at the River House and walked up to his hotel to meet him for breakfast. He was already seated in the dining room when I entered and sat down and ordered the big breakfast.

"How did you sleep?" I asked.

"Not bad. Traveling always tires me out."

"Well if you're not too tired tonight you can catch the Jenny and Jeremy show at the theater." I told him about how we were pressed into service when the Flowers' murder had threatened to close the show.

"Oh, I'd pay double to see that."

"We actually weren't that bad."

"So when are you setting up your trap?" he said to change the subject.

"First we have to eliminate Mark Johnson as a suspect. Of course there's always the possibility that he murdered his girlfriend. Detective McKenzie agreed to let the Canadian police pick him up for questioning. We should hear from him this morning.

After breakfast we headed over to the police station to see detective McKenzie.

"I just called your hotel and left a message for you," he said to Rob as we sat down opposite his desk.

"I take it that he had an alibi and that he is still calling himself by his cousin's name of Daniel Andrews?" I asked.

"Yes, and he showed the police his identification."

"You didn't tell them his real identity, did you?"

"No. As far as they're concerned this was just a routine check. He was having breakfast and then went to a bank to set up an account at the time of the murder. His alibi checked out. He's not the murderer. However when he crosses into this country again the border police will pick him up for questioning about the missing financial documents."

"Chances are," I said, "that the bank where he opened an account can provide us with information about the certificates. If we can determine that these are the stolen papers then we can send him to jail." And I can close this case, I said to myself.

"Will the bank help us?" asked Rob. "They have no obligation to do so."

"Yes, they will, I'm sure. They don't want an international incident, even if it's a small one."

"I have a good idea about who killed Viola Flowers," I added. "But I'll need your help to prove it."

"It's highly irregular, but as a courtesy to the Boston police," McKenzie said nodding to Rob, "I think we can work with you."

It was a perfect morning as Rob and I headed out. The air was clear and the sun was warm. Walking along the street we could see the falls off in the distance. Tourists had already started to congregate near the falls to see the tourist attraction up close. We walked across the bridge to Canada and answered the brief questions at the border. The First Bank of Ontario was easy enough to find once we reached the small business section of the village which lay just outside the falls tourist area.

"The Canadian side has the best views doesn't it?" observed Rob as we walked along. This was the first time he had been in Niagara.

"Yes, but it also has more tourist traps than the American side."

"It would be fun to come here sometime when we're not working."

"Agreed," I answered.

We entered the bank and asked to speak to the bank manager. We were led into a small office off to the side of the bank lobby. The bank manager introduced himself as Mr. Thomas Jones.

"What can I do for you gentlemen?"

"I'm Lieutenant Robert Williams of the Boston Police Department, and this is Jeremy Dance, an investigator. We understand the delicacy of the situation, but we think that an American has opened an account with you using stolen bonds from a Boston financial institution. What makes this more critical is that murder may have been involved."

"Oh, my," said Mr. Jones looking quite distressed. "Under the circumstance I'll try to help if I can."

"Did a gentleman named either Daniel Andrews or Mark Johnson open an account using certificates bearing the name of Brigham Financial Services?" I asked.

"Give me a few minutes and I'll check with my staff," he said as he left the office.

"Bearer certificates are usually not traceable," I said to Rob. "Which is the point of them, I suppose."

"Not all the papers were bonds. We only need one thing to tie Johnson to the theft."

"If he murdered his cousin, then theft is the least of his problems."

Through the open door we could see Jones conferring with the tellers and managers. I saw him stop at a desk and the manager nodding as they conferred. "I think we have a hit," I said as Jones came scurrying back.

"My floor manager," said Mr. Jones as he entered the office, "opened an account for a Mark Johnson yesterday, and he used bearer bonds and other certificates."

"It's interesting," I observed, "that he used his real name."

"Considering that everyone thinks that Mark Johnson of Boston is dead, it's not so risky," said Rob.

"This may help," said Mr. Jones as he placed a sheet of paper in front of us. "This is a letter of credit that's been written on Brigham Financial Services letter head."

"I'll wager it's a forgery, and if it is we've enough to arrest him," said Rob. "Thank you, Mr. Jones. You and your bank have been most helpful."

"Now what?" I asked as we headed back across the river.

"I'll get in touch with detective McKenzie and we'll get a warrant to pick up Johnson. As soon as he steps across the border he'll be detained."

"I'll have to tell Cora Andrews that her missing husband was the one who died in the fire and not his cousin."

"You should probably wait until we pick up Johnson. Hopefully he can confirm that the body was Andrews."

"Yes, you're probably right," I agreed. I looked at my watch. "How about lunch after we stop off to see McKenzie? Then Jenny and I have to rehearse for tonight's performance."

"I can't wait to see that," said Rob with a smile. "You better be good."

"I assure you. We are wonderful!"

Detective McKenzie was impressed that we had managed to get proof that Mark Johnson was in possession of the stolen bonds since it's very hard to trace bearer bonds. Fortunately we had the credit letter, which I was pretty sure was forged.

"If he's smart he'll stay in Canada," said Rob.

"The good thing about criminals," said McKenzie, "is that they are rarely smart."

"Very true," confirmed Rob.

"If he doesn't show up in the next few days, I'll contact the Canadian authorities, and we can get him extradited." McKenzie had a very determined look on his face. "I still need to find out who killed the Flowers dame."

"With any luck I can uncover the murderer tomorrow morning," I said with more bravado than I felt. I pretty much knew who did it, but I needed to prove it.

"I think you're enjoying this," I said to Jenny as we waited in the wings of the Opera House to go on.

"I am enjoying it. So are you. When was the last time you got to perform in a place this large?"

"Never," I answered. "This is taking being undercover to a whole new extreme."

"I think you're nervous because Rob is in the audience."

"I think you might be right," I said as the stage manager signaled us to go on stage.

Chapter 14

Jenny, Rob, and I had a late supper after the theater and got back to the hotel around one. I sat in my room and wrote out three identical notes to slip under the doors of my three suspects. The note said simply:

> *I know what you've done and it's going to cost you...Meet me at the Niagara Diner at ten tomorrow.*
>
> *A friend*

Somehow I knew Mark Johnson, or as he was known by his dead cousin's name Dan Andrews, was mixed up in it somehow. He posed as a rich guy from New York in order to impress Viola Flowers. Someone was jealous. Was it her sister? Was she jealous that Viola had a rich boy friend and she didn't? Was it Mary Marguerite Burke? Did she want Dan for herself? Or was it Jim Hammond. Was the manager in love with Viola and did she lead him on? My money was on Hammond, but I wasn't a good gambler.

I sat in a booth at the diner with my back to the nearby door and a cup of coffee in my hand. There was a mirror over the lunch counter, and I could see the door from there. I took out my watch and saw that it was ten past ten when my guest walked through the door.

"Have a seat," I said to my guest.

"Oh, Jeremy, thanks. But I'm meeting someone."

"Dan Andrews isn't coming," I said. "In fact there's no such person. His real name is Mark Johnson and he's a thief. Now sit down."

Mary Marguerite Burke sat down.

"I really didn't think it was you," I said. "But now it all makes sense,"

"What are you talking about?"

"You killed Viola Flowers."

"You're crazy. Viola was alive when we left for our walk. I was with you. And then I went to the theater. I have witnesses."

"I haven't forgotten that you're a ventriloquist. It wasn't Viola speaking on the other side of the door that morning. You had killed her earlier and then used your voice to make us all believe that she was alive. Did you plan to kill her or was it an accident?"

Suddenly she slumped down and looked defeated. "It was an accident, I swear. We were arguing, and she tripped and hit her head. I panicked."

"You should turn yourself in," I said. "It will look better if you do it and not me."

"I'll go to the police station right now."

"No need," I said and gestured to the two men sitting at the counter. One of them was Ken McKenzie. "These gentlemen are with the police, and they'll be happy to escort you. For the record

Detective McKenzie, Miss Burke is turning herself in."

"So noted. Thanks Mr. Dance." Mary Marguerite looked at me confused. "I'm not Mr. Smith. I'm a private detective."

"It really was an accident." She was sobbing uncontrollably.

"I'll find you a good lawyer," I said. I was about to leave when McKenzie stopped me.

"Customs picked up Mark Johnson an hour ago. Your friend Rob Williams is over there now."

This was great news. The sooner I could wrap it up here, the sooner I could get to work on my next case.

"This is partly your case, too," said Ken McKenzie as he escorted me into the interrogation room. "And I owe you for identifying the Flowers killer."

"Thanks, Ken." Mark Johnson was seated at a metal table in the small interview room. A single overhead light was directed at Johnson. Rob was already seated and a stenographer was ready to take notes.

"You don't seem very broken up about your girlfriend," Rob said.

"Hey, it was nothing serious. We just shared a few laughs. I didn't even know about it until they picked me up for questioning. Tough break for her."

"Your concern is overwhelming," remarked McKenzie with a note of irony.

"Thanks," said Johnson clearly missing the irony.

"Tell us about the papers you stole," I said getting to the point.

"You can't prove anything."

"What I can prove," I said as I showed him the letter of credit, "is that you forged this letter. I called Brigham Financial Services, and they never issued a letter of credit to you. So even if we can't legally charge you with possession of stolen bearer bonds, we've got you with intent to defraud."

"But that's not your biggest problem," added Rob. "We have the unexplained death of your cousin in your apartment. Very convenient that he died in the fire, and everyone assumed it was you. How did you kill him?"

For the first time Johnson showed some emotion. "I didn't kill Dan. He was staying at my place to get away from that god-awful wife of his. He was a smoker. He must have fallen asleep. I admit to stealing the papers, but I didn't know anything about the fire until later."

"And how did you get hold of his money?"

"I didn't take his money. The money must have burned with him."

"When did you get the idea to steal Dan Andrews's identity?" asked McKenzie.

"Not until I read about the fire in the paper. The story said it was me who died. I saw an opportunity and I took it."

"I'm arresting you," said Rob, "for fraud, theft, and hindering and investigation. As soon as I can get the paperwork together, you and I are going back to Boston."

Rob stayed in Niagara until he could get the extradition papers together. Jenny and I checked out of the River House and caught the next train out.

"Admit it," I said to her on the trip back. "You had a good time with this investigation."

"This was so much more interesting than my usual divorce cases."

"And I have to admit that playing at being performers was fun. However, now I have to go back and tell Cora Andrews that her husband is dead."

"She hired you to find the truth and you did. I suspect she knew in her heart that he was dead."

"I think I'll leave out the part about his running away from her. It wouldn't help anything at this point."

Jenny and I parted company in New York City and I journeyed on to Boston. Roscoe was waiting for me at South Station.

"Welcome back, Mr. Jeremy."

"Good to see you Roscoe and good to be home. What did you find out in Philadelphia?"

106

"I didn't find out a lot," he said as he loaded my bags into the car, "But here's an interesting fact. Ina Patterson's first husband, Jacob Jones, died of natural causes according to the death certificate, but there was no autopsy."

"That's not so unusual," I said.

"Except he was only forty."

"That is a little young," I said once we were in the car. "I was under the impression that they were all old men. But that still doesn't really mean anything. Lots of guys have heart attacks in their forties."

"But," added Roscoe, "the doctor who wrote out the death certificate became Ina Patterson's next husband."

Chapter 15

Jimmy Kirk was at the front door to take my hat when I arrived back home on Beacon Hill. "Welcome back, sir. Miss Velda called to invite you to dinner tonight."

"How did she know I was back?"

"I may have told her when she called earlier," answered Roscoe as he headed for the kitchen.

I really was looking forward to having a quiet evening at home and really didn't feel like having dinner with a bunch of Velda's friends. I picked up the phone.

"Who's coming?" I asked without preamble.

"Hello, Jeremy. Nice of you to call."

I waited without comment.

"It will just be the two of us. I want to hear all about your adventures, darling. I'm so bored. Be here at eight."

"Fine," I said and hung up. I might have been a little too abrupt. I decided to stop and get some flowers first. I looked at the clock and realized I had time to go and see Cora Andrews. I dreaded giving her the bad news. I decided to drive myself and had Roscoe bring the car around.

The late afternoon traffic was heavy as I headed toward Charles Street, past Mass General Hospital and across the bridge into Cambridge. I had to dodge several trolleys in Cambridge as I headed toward Cora Andrews house. The colored maid who answered the door recognized me, and I thought she looked a little disappointed when she didn't see Roscoe. She took me into a small study.

"I'll inform Mrs. Andrews that you're here. And next time bring your man with you," she giggled and left. Roscoe had made quite an impression.

"Mr. Dance, how kind of you to call," said Cora as she swept into the room. She was wearing a colorful print afternoon outfit fit for a garden party. "Have you news for me?"

"Please sit down, Mrs. Andrews," I said. "I'm afraid the news isn't good." I told her the facts of the case, leaving out the fact that Dan Andrews was indeed running away. She listened without expression.

"Thank you Mr. Dance for your hard work. It is just as I feared. Please send me your bill. You've been very helpful. Now I can move on in my life."

She didn't show any emotion as I prepared to leave. "If I can be of any further assistance, please feel free to call," I said as I rose from my seat. "I can see myself out."

"The flowers are lovely, Jeremy," said Velda as she passed them to her maid to place in a vase.

"Is that one of your paintings?" I asked as we headed into the parlor. "I don't recall seeing it before." It was a rather abstract landscape that picked up on the colors of the room and looked perfect over the mantle.

"I couldn't decide what to put there, so I painted it to match the room."

"It's wonderful," I remarked. "Have you set up your Maine studio yet?"

"I've had everything shipped there that I need. I've hired a local girl to go in and clean, and I've got the island handyman doing some repairs."

"When are you going?"

"I'll leave on Monday. I want you and Rob to come and visit. There's the Island Inn where you'll be quite comfortable, and it's a five minute walk to my studio."

"Tell me about the island."

"It's a small island off the Maine coast about five miles out to sea. The nearest large towns are Boothbay Harbor and Rockland. Many of the summer residents are artist and the year-rounders are mostly fishermen and their families."

"Sounds very quaint."

"Say you'll come?"

"Of course."

"Where are my manners? I should offer you a drink."

"A drink," I said. "would be most welcome." I gave her a quick version of my Niagara trip and the outcome of my investigation."

"That must have been tough to give bad news," she said referring to my visit to Cora Andrews. "But I want to hear more about your vaudeville debut."

As soon as I finished my story the maid entered to announce dinner. We finished our drinks and headed toward the dining room. After the soup course I sat back and looked at her.

"Now tell me why I'm really here?"

"Father wants to come for a visit."

"No," I said.

"Now Jeremy..."

"No!"

"It's been three years since we've seen him."

"Ask me in another three years."

"He wants to see you."

"He said that?"

"Yes, he did."

"Is he bringing that bitch with him?"

"Actually he isn't."

I looked at her.

"He's divorcing her?"

"Really he is. He said he wants to make amends."

"We'll see." I didn't really believe it.

"So you'll see him."

"If it will keep you from nagging me, I suppose so." I knew once Velda set her mind to something there was no way she would let it drop. "When is the happy reunion?"

"Not until next month, so don't worry."

"If he can find the time," I added.

"That's true. We'll see if he really shows up."

Roscoe and I sat in my study looking over the file on Ina Patterson. Nora Wilde had hired us to check her background fearing that her father might be in danger since Ina's previous marriages had ended tragically.

"The first thing that I need to know is who is telling the truth. According to Miss Wilde her parents were devoted to each other. Emma Goodwin, who is the eyes and ears of Beacon Hill swears that they loathed each other," I sat back at my desk and fiddled with my pencil.

"What I've noticed about people," said Roscoe sitting at his smaller desk, "is that there can be a difference between how people treat each other and how they really feel."

"Appearance versus reality?"

"Yes, like you and Mr. Rob. To the casual observer you are old chums from school who've kept in touch. The reality is that you two…"

"Yes, I see your point."

"What I don't understand," said Roscoe, "is what difference it makes in the case. We're looking at Ina Patterson's relationships, not Mr. Wilde's."

"In addition to the death of Ina's three husbands, there is also the sudden death of Liddy Wilde on a train."

Roscoe looked at me for a few moments. "I see your point."

"Anyway, here is what we know so far. She's forty-eight years old and has been married three times. The first time in Philadelphia in 1908 at the age of twenty. Her husband died a year later of an apparent heart attack, but no autopsy was performed. Two years later she married the doctor who signed the late husband's death certificate."

"Sounds suspicious to me," remarked Roscoe.

"It's odd at the very least. Then the good doctor passed away a few years later. We don't know anything about his death at all."

"What I learned about him in my trip to Philadelphia," added Roscoe, "was that they moved to New York City after they were married. He joined the staff at Bellevue Hospital."

"New York City? I'll put in a call to Jenny Johnson and have her check out Bellevue, though there may not be many who remember him from 1912. Do we know anything about his death?"

"Not yet. But I bet Mrs. Johnson can find out."

"I'm counting on it," I said as I picked up the phone.

Myra Pennington was in town, and I made a point to invite her for lunch. Myra started out her career as a society columnist for the *Boston Post*. She had helped me out on a previous case, and I had given her an exclusive. She was now a Washington correspondent and her column was carried by the wire services. Judy and Myra were lovers, but the separation was difficult on Judy. I didn't want to intrude on their time, but I needed to see Myra alone. Since Judy rarely got up before ten, I asked Myra to meet me for breakfast at The Back Bay Grill.

Myra was already seated when I arrived. "You're early. I thought I'd beat you. It's good to see you Myra."

"It's good to see you, too, Jeremy." She got up and gave me a hug. I ordered coffee and eggs and bacon. Myra had tea and cinnamon toast.

"How's Washington treating you?" I asked.

"Oh, Jeremy, I love it. It's so exciting. I've even had lunch with Mrs. Roosevelt."

"That does sound interesting. What's she like?"

"She's very smart. She actually thinks things through to the end. She's a great supporter of women workers. What have you been up to? How's Rob? And what's Velda doing?"

Breakfast arrived and I did my best to answer her questions. I got the impression that as much as she loved Washington, she missed Boston.

"As much as I love seeing you, Jeremy, I know you, and you've got something on your mind."

"Yes, I need your help. You were a society editor for many years. I need some background on the Wilde family."

"I think I can help there. I know Nora Wilde, but not well. I still have some society contacts. What do you need to know?"

"Liddy Wilde died suddenly on a trip to New York. I've heard conflicting reports about their marriage. I'd like you to see if you can find out the truth."

"And what's in it for me?" she looked at me across the table.

"If there is a story in this somewhere, and I'm not saying that there is, you'll get the story first."

"It's a deal," she said.

Chapter 16

Mark Johnson was locked up in the Charles Street Jail. Rob had facilitated the transfer from New York to Boston and I hoped it would be a long time before Johnson saw the light of day. He had caused too many problems for too many people and I wasn't at all certain that he was innocent of his cousin's death. At any rate, my involvement with the case was at an end, or so I thought.

I must have fallen asleep in my easy chair. It was a warm evening, and the windows were open. There was a gentle rain falling and the sound must have lulled me to sleep. I didn't hear Rob come in, but I felt a hand gently stroking my hair.

"When did you get in?" I asked, yawning as I looked up.

"A few minutes ago, I didn't want to disturb you."

"You disturb me all the time."

"I know, and I enjoy it."

I could tell by looking at him that he had something to say.

"You'll never guess who bailed out Mark Johnson," Rob said looking like he couldn't wait to tell me.

"He made bail?"

"Yes, and Cora Andrews paid for it."

"What?"

"She bailed him out."

"But he might be her husband's killer and if nothing else he obstructed the investigation of the fire."

"Not really. We just assumed that the body was Johnson's. The only thing we can prove is that he used a dead man's identity to defraud."

"Do you think Cora Andrews is involved?" I asked. "Never mind, I'm pretty sure she is somehow." Cora had hired me to find her missing husband, and it's very possible that she knew he was dead. That at least explained her rather subdued reaction when I told her that her husband was the one who died in the fire.

"Well, without evidence there's nothing much we can do."

"There's nothing much the police can do," I answered. "I don't have those limitations. I hate when someone tries to use me for their schemes."

"You're going to make an issue out of this aren't you?"

"You bet I am. Cora Andrews is in for a rough ride. Lucky for her I have another case to work on or she be 'discomforted' much sooner."

"How about if I take you out to dinner?" asked Rob.

"That's a great idea. And then?"

"And then, indeed!"

I opened my eyes and tried to take charge of my sleep-addled brain. Rob was half-dressed and standing over me. "What are you doing?" I asked.

"In case you have forgotten, I work for the City of Boston, and I have to go to work."

"How tiresome," I yawned.

"We can't all be rich men about town."

"Actually, you are almost as rich as I am."

"Oh, yes, that's right. Sometimes I forget," he said laughing. "Get up and have breakfast with me."

"Fine, but I'm not getting dressed."

"Even better,"

Roscoe had our breakfast ready as we made our way to the dining room.

"What's on the calendar today, Roscoe?" I asked.

"You're having lunch with Miss Hogarth and Miss Pennington. And then you're having tea with Mrs. Goodwin."

"I am?"

"Yes, Mrs. Goodwin called earlier. I had the feeling that it was more than a request."

"I see," I answered. "Any chance you can join me, Rob?"

"Not on your life."

"Thanks." I said as I filled my coffee cup and tucked into my breakfast.

The morning gave me an opportunity to get some paperwork done at my desk and get caught up on correspondence. By the time I finished at my desk it was only ten-thirty and I had an hour and a half wait until I met the ladies for lunch. It was a nice morning for a walk. Not too hot and not rainy for once.

I headed down Beacon Hill to Charles Street and over to the Boston Commons. I wasn't the only one out for a stroll as the benches were full and the paths crowded. I was able to find an unoccupied bench under a tree in the Public Gardens that had a view of the swan boats. I needed some time to think.

I was still deeply disturbed about Cora Andrews and Mark Johnson and their possible complicity in the death of Dan Andrews. If they had used me in their scheme, I'm afraid they'd have to pay the price. Still, I had to be sure.

Before I could devote any time to that situation, I had an actual case to work on. I had much more to learn about Ina Patterson. I'd have to check in with Nora Wilde as soon as possible, but it seemed my day was already filled up for today. I couldn't help but wonder why Emma Goodwin had summoned me to her home on Mt. Vernon Street. I had to laugh. Mt Vernon was now a respectable neighborhood; but in the not too distant past it had been nicknamed Mt. Whoredom as it was Boston's red light district.

I took out my pocket watch and saw that it was time to head over to the Parker House for lunch. Traffic was especially heavy around the commons as I headed over to School Street.

"I'll be joined by two ladies," I told the head waiter as he seated me in the dining room. I ordered a cocktail and sat back to look around. The crowd was affluent and provided an atmosphere of color and romance. The liveried waiters were efficient and the notes from the piano drifted out over the animated conversation of the diners. The room was filling up quickly when I was joined by Judy and Myra.

"How kind of you to invite us to lunch," said Myra as she and Judy were seated by the head waiter.

"Yes," added Judy. "I hardly see you anymore."

"Judy told me about how you saved those poor workers from being swindled. I would have loved to see you dressed as a tramp."

"He was quite convincing," laughed Judy.

The waiter took their drink orders and gave us menus to peruse.

"I can't tell you how much I miss Boston," sighed Myra. "Washington is exciting, but I really don't know it well enough, and it doesn't feel like home."

"You could come back anytime," said Judy.

"And you could come to Washington."

"Maybe I will," answered Judy just as the waiter came to take our order. I ordered a nice porter house steak. I told myself I had to keep up my strength for tea with Emma Goodwin. The ladies were more restrained in their lunch choices. Judy ordered a cob salad and Myra ordered fillet of sole with a light cream sauce.

"I do have some information for you, Jeremy," said Myra as soon as the waiter left.

"You're a peach, Myra. What is it?"

"I visited several of my old friends yesterday. According to my sources, the Wilde marriage was not a happy one."

"Who are your sources?" asked Judy.

"You know I can't reveal my sources. Let's just say they were close friends of the couple."

"I see," that seemed to satisfy Judy.

"Go on," I said and gave Judy a dirty look.

"Well, according to my sources. Liddy and Cornelius Wilde were involved in a bitter divorce case."

"What?" This was the first I was hearing about it. I'd have to have a little talk with Nora.

"It was all very, very discrete. She wasn't just taking a trip to New York, she was leaving Cornelius."

"And she died on the train to New York. Very convenient."

"That's what I was thinking," replied Myra.

"Thanks, Myra. You've been very helpful." Our lunches arrived and for the rest of the meal we talked about the happenings of Boston and Washington.

Beacon Hill contains some of the oldest houses in Boston. Both the streets and houses are narrow, and the trees are ancient. The Back Bay, by comparison, is much newer, with larger houses and straighter streets. Boston was once a town with three hills, but the hills had been cut away and the soil used to fill in the Back Bay. Mt. Vernon Street was no longer a large hill, but it was still a hill.

By the time I reached Emma Goodwin's Townhouse I was sweating. The weather had turned hot and humid. I was admitted by the maid and taken into Emma's sitting room. The windows were closed and the drapes were drawn, but the effect was to make the room much cooler.

"Jeremy dear, please have a seat. Betsy, please bring Mr. Dance a nice gin and tonic." She looked at me questioning, and I nodded my head.

"A gin and tonic would be most welcome."

We began with the obligatory observations of the weather and questions about our mutual health. Betsy returned with the gin and tonics and left the room.

"I had a nice letter from George Van Clef."

"My father? I see," I said and took a long gulp of my drink. I wasn't expecting this conversation.

"He is getting rid of that terrible woman and wants to make amends with his children. He's asked me to help."

"You? Why?"

"I said I'd help. Your mother was very dear to me and I know this rift would have broken her heart."

"I didn't cause the rift," I said defending myself. "He disowned me."

"No one blames you, Jeremy. But you have to realize your little indiscretion was a bit of a shock." The little "indiscretion" that she was talking about was the scandal of Rob and me getting kicked out of the service on moral grounds. It cost both our families money to keep it quiet.

"That's not the way it felt. I had to move away and change my name."

"And that was a choice you made. Though I would have done the same thing, I have to say."

"What's your interest in all this?" I asked point blank.

"I'm planning a small dinner party at the end of the month. I've asked your father to attend, and I want you and Velda to be here."

"I don't know about…"

"Jeremy!"

"Fine. We'll be here." This was the second time the subject had come up and I couldn't fight both Velda and Emma.

Chapter 17

Nora Wilde sat in the red chair in my office. She had a handkerchief in her hand that she was unconsciously twisting. I could tell that she was nervous, and I had no intention of putting her at ease.

"Miss Wilde," I said sharply. "When I take a case I expect my client to be completely honest with me. You have not been."

"What do you mean?"

"I mean that you lied about certain facts concerning your parents. You told me they were devoted to each other. Now I find out that they were in the middle of a bitter divorce."

"No one knows about that," she said looking shocked.

"Apparently they do. And I have to remind you that divorce is no longer the scandal it once was."

"I didn't tell you," she said sounding defensive, "because I asked you to look into Ina Patterson's background. Not my parents."

"I need all the information. Even the smallest detail you think is insignificant might have importance. So I want you to tell me everything. If I find out that you're withholding anything then I'm going to drop the case."

"Please don't," she begged.

"Then you'll tell me everything?"

"Yes," she said nodding her head.

"So you better start at the beginning."

"My parents were devoted to each other. At least they were. Something changed about three years ago. Suddenly they were barely speaking, and my father started leaving home on business trips for long periods of time."

"Have you any idea what caused the rift?"

"I'm sure it was Ina Patterson."

"What makes you think that?"

"My mother and Ina were friends, but she hadn't seen or heard from Ina for years. One day she just appeared and after that things were never the same between my parents."

"Interesting," I said. I really didn't know what to make of it. "So how did your father get involved with Ina?"

"When my mother died, Ina stepped in and claimed that my mother told her that her heart was not good and that they had talked about funeral plans should anything happen. My father was relieved that Ina was willing to do the funeral planning."

"Did you know your mother had heart trouble?"

"No, and neither did my father."

"Who was her doctor?"

"James Flannery over at Mass General." Flannery was one of the top doctors in Boston.

"I know Dr. Flannery," I said. James was a member of the Windsor Club and we'd often exchanged pleasantries over drinks.

125

"I'm not sure what my mother has to do with any of this," Nora Wilde was looking confused.

"I don't either," I admitted. "But I think I need to have a talk with Dr. Flannery.

As soon as Nora left I picked up the phone and called Lyle Compton the manager of the Windsor Club. I asked him about Dr. Flannery's habits.

"This is highly irregular," said Compton. "We don't keep track of our members."

"The hell you don't," I said. "Don't bull shit me. And you owe me a favor." I reminded him.

"He comes in promptly at five for cocktails and usually stays for dinner."

"That's better," I said and hung up. James Flannery, I knew, was single and like many single professionals he took his meals out. I rang the bell next to my desk.

"Yes, sir?" Jimmy Kirk stood in the doorway.

"Jimmy, Mr. Williams and I will be dining out tonight. You may take the night off."

"Yes, thank you, sir." Jimmy was grinning ear to ear.

The bar at the Windsor Club was at one end of the lounge. It was a traditional looking bar of dark chestnut wood and brass rails. Above the bar was a mural of men gathered at a swimming hole getting ready to swim in the all-together. The whole club was decorated with paintings of male art, all tastefully rendered, you understand.

I sat in the corner where I could keep an eye on the bar and the door as I read through one of the newspapers. Rob came into the lounge, saw me, and took a seat next to me.

"What's going on?" he asked.

"We're going to ply James Flannery with drink when he comes in."

"Why?"

"Information."

"I see. I was hoping for a quiet evening at home. Maybe listen to the radio and go to bed early."

"With any luck I can get the information I need and then we can head home."

"There he is now," Rob said as we both watched him come in and head for the bar. Drink in hand he turned around to look for a seat. Flannery was around thirty and extremely handsome, which attracted middle-aged women to his practice. I waved at him and he came over and took a seat.

"Good to see you both," he said. "I don't see you around much anymore."

"My man has the night off, so Rob and I thought we'd eat here. Would you care to join us?"

"Thank you, yes. It gets tedious to eat alone. Or even worse is dining with some of our more wearisome members."

"I couldn't agree more."

"Jeremy and I need to socialize more," said Rob. "We get so wrapped up in our work that our social life suffers."

"I can understand that. My patients take up most of my time."

"I'm actually working on a case that involves one of your former patients." I didn't expect to find an opening so early in the conversation.

"Really? May I ask who?"

"I really need to respect confidentiality." I said. James looked disappointed. This was going to be easier than I thought it would be. "But since we're both professionals and understand the code of confidentiality, I'm sure it would be alright if both of us shared information and promised that it wouldn't leave this room."

"Yes, that sounds reasonable."

I looked at my watch. "Let's discuss this over dinner," I suggested.

"An excellent idea," agreed James. Rob, who had watched me work on James Flannery, gave me a wink as we got up to head to the dining room.

The room was dimly lit. Soft electric lights had replaced the candles as a concession to summer. Ceiling fans created a gentle breeze and freshly cut flowers adorned each table.

Our favorite waiter practically tripped over himself coming over to our table. I couldn't blame him as we were the only men here under the age of seventy. He passed us the hand-lettered menus and went to fetch us ice water.

"I should offer to give him a free exam," observed James.

"After Jeremy and I take him home for police interrogation," replied Rob.

"Behave yourselves," I laughed. The ice water arrived, and we ordered another round of cocktails. The waiter took our orders and we resumed our conversation.

"Liddy Wilde was a patient of yours was she not?" I asked.

"Yes, she was. Don't tell me you're looking into her death?"

"Not exactly. I'm working for her daughter." I went on and explained the case.

"How can I help?"

"According to the daughter, her mother died of a heart attack."

"That was the conclusion of the New York coroner."

"Did she have a bad heart?"

"Liddy Wilde was as healthy as a horse. I couldn't believe that she died."

"So what is your professional opinion?" asked Rob.

"It's not unheard of for a middle aged woman to have a heart attack. It's rare, but it does happen. Usually there are contributing factors."

"Such as?" I asked.

"Usually excessive weight, lack of exercise and fresh air, and sometimes a nervous disposition. And Liddy Wilde had none of those."

"I see, I said.

"So it came as quite a shock when I learned she had died."

"Is it possible," asked Rob, "that it wasn't a heart attack?"

"What do you mean?"

"I mean," continued Rob, "is it possible that she died of some other cause? Could something like poison mimic a heart attack?"

"I suppose it's possible. But poison usually can be spotted by a coroner. I'm quite confident that she died of a heart attack."

"How about her mental or emotional state?" I asked.

"Liddy Wilde wasn't just physically strong. She was a force of nature."

We finished dinner, and I realized that I hadn't really learned anything that would be helpful. At least that's what I thought at the time.

Chapter 18

The next morning was bright and clear and there was a cool sea breeze that promised to keep Beacon Hill from sweltering in the heat wave that had hit New York City. Last summer had been brutally hot in Boston, and I had to exile myself to the mountains of New Hampshire.

Rob was taking an early shift, and I walked part way with him to enjoy the fresh air. We stopped for breakfast at a small city diner by Mass General. The diner was crowded with hospital workers on their way to work. Even in a depression there was no shortage of sickness. When I returned home Roscoe greeted me at the door hopping from one leg to the other, and I didn't need to be a detective to know he had some news.

"What is it Roscoe?"

"Mrs. Goodwin called earlier. She said she was going to call on Ina Patterson and needed an escort."

"Perfect! What time?"

"She asked if you could pick her up around one."

"Cancel whatever is on the calendar for this afternoon, Roscoe. I've got a date."

"Nice costume," I said to Roscoe as he held the car door open for me. On occasion when I have to make an appearance I have Roscoe dress in a chauffeur's uniform.

131

"Got to love a man in uniform."

We picked Emma Goodwin up at her home and headed out to Brookline where Ina had a small "cottage."

"Some slum," I said as we rolled up to the house. It was a brick Tudor-style house with a large garden. I estimated that it probably had at least six bedrooms.

"Ina likes to marry well," replied Emma as I helped her out of the car.

"And often, apparently."

The house had what would be considered an English Garden with lots of delphiniums, foxglove, columbine, impatiens, and many flowers that I couldn't identify. The whole effect was a riot of color.

"I'm impressed," said Emma as she looked around.

"Me, too." I agreed.

"Before we go in Jeremy, I think it would be best if you used your real name and not Dance, since she was a classmate of your mother's. We wouldn't want to tip her off."

"I suppose," I reluctantly agreed, although I knew she was right. Ina's maid answered the door, took my hat, and showed us into Ina's drawing room. Ina swept into the room dressed in a silk summer dress. Her blonde hair was waved, and I had to admit that she looked about ten years younger than her age.

"Mrs. Goodwin what a pleasure," she said as she greeted us. She turned to me and gave me a smile.

"This is Mr. Van Clef of Philadelphia," said Emma as she introduced us. "He was kind enough to accompany me here."

"Van Clef?" Ina repeated. "The name does ring a bell. But I can't place it."

"You have a lovely home," said Emma to change the subject. Indeed it was. The English cottage look extended inside and the effect was warm and cozy if a bit overdone. The room was a riot of color. The wallpaper pattern had large red cabbage roses and the color was picked up by the floral drapes and rug. The upholstery was striped red and blue.

Just then an elderly woman with a cane walked into the room.

"Come in, Mildred," said Ina. "I want you to meet our guests. This is Mrs. Emma Goodwin and Mr. Jeremy Van Clef. Mildred Blasdell had agreed to be my companion."

"How do you do," said Miss Blasdell. We shook hands all around. "Ina has taken pity on an old woman and given me a place to live."

"Oh, how kind," remarked Emma.

"I've been so lonely since my husband died. It's been nice to have someone in the house," Ina added."

I wanted to ask which husband, but I thought better of it. "I couldn't help but admire your front garden," I said. "I'm quite a landscape enthusiast."

"Then let me show you the backyard garden. I'll have lemonade brought out to us." Ina picked up a bell and rang it. She gave orders to the maid, and we followed her outside through the french doors to a small grapevine covered arbor that offered comfortable seating and shade from the sun. Miss Blasdell, for her part, decided to stay in the cool of the house.

"I designed the garden myself," she said as she pointed out the various sections of her backyard. "Over there," she said pointing to the back, "I have a small vegetable garden and next to it is a small herb garden. Do you garden, Mr. Van Clef?"

"I have a small garden behind my house, but I'm afraid that my front garden consists only of window boxes."

"I've only just heard," said Emma Goodwin, "that you are to be congratulated on you engagement."

"Thank you. I've been lucky in love again. Cornelius Wilde is quite a find if I do say so."

Emma, never one to be subtle, looked at her and said, "You've had such tragic ending to your marriages, I hope you have better luck this time."

"Yes," replied Ina looking somewhat taken aback. "I do hope so."

"Lose another one, Ina, and people will talk." Emma chuckled at her own joke. Ina went white as a sheet, but managed a laugh.

"May I look around your garden?" I asked. I thought it best to let the ladies talk.

"Certainly Mr. Van Clef."

I knew Emma and Ina would share gossip as soon as I was out of ear shot. It was Emma's way to get her victims to open up. The garden was magnificent. Here the same flowers as the front garden were planted, but instead of the undisciplined English garden, the backyard was more formal with classic placements. The vegetable garden was fenced off with a small white picket fence and the herb garden was walled in by granite rocks. Here too, I was only able to identify half of the plants.

I slowly made my way back toward the arbor where I could hear laughter. As soon as I approached it became quiet.

"Lovely to see you again, Ina," said Emma Goodwin as she rose from her seat. "I fear I've kept Mr. Van Clef away from his home far too long."

"Thank you for stopping by," said Ina. "Pleased to meet you Mr. Van Clef."

The maid retrieved my hat, and I helped Emma into the car.

"What did you learn?" I asked her as I slid into the back seat and signaled Roscoe to take off.

"I learned that she thinks you'd be a good match for her future step-daughter."

"Nora Wilde?' I laughed.

"I didn't discourage it," Emma replied. "It might be a handy rouse sometime."

"Perhaps. What else did you learn?"

"She thinks Nora doesn't like her."

"That's an understatement if there ever was one."

"At least you got a chance to meet her and form your own opinion."

"She's very beautiful," I conceded. "And very charming. Neither of which rules her out as a husband killer."

The evening was warm and Rob and I sat listening to the radio. The news was alarming. The heat wave that had started out in the Southwest had moved steadily into the Midwest. Steele, North Dakota, had recorded the highest temperature ever at 121 degrees. The prediction was that the heat wave would make its way slowly to the Northeast. So far the heat wave has killed over four thousand.

"We'll have to head up into the mountains," I said to Rob.

"You'll have to finish up your investigation soon then."

"It's hot today. Can you imagine Boston when it's 100 degrees or more?"

"Don't even think it. The warmer it gets the crazier people get."

Roscoe can into the room. "Mrs. Johnson on the phone for you, Mr. Jeremy."

"Thank you, Roscoe. I'll take it up in my office."

"Jenny, good of you to call," I said into the receiver.

"Jeremy, I just wanted you to know that I finished my investigation into Ina Patterson's second husband. I typed up the report and put it in the mail. You should get it in a day or two."

"Any surprises?"

"I think you'll find it interesting reading."

"Great. Send me the bill and we'll settle up."

"Thanks Jeremy. Working with you has been fun."

I rang off and headed back to the parlor where Rob was intently listening to the radio. He gave me a questioning look.

"That was Jenny Johnson. She is sending me some interesting reading about Ina Patterson."

"This case is beginning to seem a little more involved than your usual cases."

"Every time I unlock a door there always seems to be two more doors to unlock."

"Maybe I should become a policeman. Most of your murders are easy to figure out. A killed B and left C for evidence."

"You might have simplified it too much, but basically you are right."

Chapter 19

Rob and I stood outside looking up at the boarded up apartment building. We were meeting with the city fire investigator, Billy Bradshaw, who was a friend of ours. Billy was a huge man who must have been about six-seven and built like a football player. We had asked him to meet us at the site of the Huntington Avenue fire that had killed Mark Andrews.

"What do you hope to find up there?" he asked as he turned to Rob.

"We're looking for evidence of a crime."

"And what is your interest in this?" he asked me.

"I was working on a case involving the dead man."

"I see. You realize you're taking a risk going into the building?"

"Sure," I said as I waved my hand in a gesture of dismissal.

"Okay then, follow me." Billy pulled out a set of keys and tried them in the padlocked front door. Most of the fire damage had been on the top floor where Mark Andrews had died. The lower floors were untouched by the fire, but were uninhabitable because of the water damage. The stench of fire damage reached my nostrils and was so strong I could almost taste it. The electricity to the building had been turned off and the only light in the stairwell was coming from an open hole in the roof where a skylight had been.

We came prepared with flashlights, and we carefully climbed the stairs to the top floor. The smell of smoke was stronger up here.

"Be careful of the floor," said Billy as he reached the top of the stairwell. The whole top floor is unstable."

"It doesn't look as bad as I thought it would," I said as I swung my flashlight around. Though everything was charred and blackened, I could make out what used to be rooms. What was left of the charred ceiling had fallen on the floor, and we had to wade through the debris as we made our way into the apartment.

"Where was the body found?" asked Rob.

"Over there," said Billy as he shone his light in a dark corner, "in what used to be the bedroom." We made our way over to the corner. The fire damage was much greater here, which according to the investigators was where the fire started.

"It seems strange that the floor is mostly undamaged and that the upper part of the room is charred," I said.

"Fire tends to burn upward, of course and the fire started on the bed. What are you looking for?" Billy asked as Rob began to carefully sift through the ashes on the floor.

"I won't know until I find it. But I believe there must be a clue here somewhere that will give us more information."

I knelt down and followed Rob's lead by taking a stick and poking through the ashes. I found a melted heap of metal which used to be an alarm clock. Every time I disturbed an ash pile I unleashed more dust in the air.

"This is interesting," said Rob as he picked up something and held it in his hand. Though it was twisted and cracked by the heat, it appeared to be a woman's locket. "I'm taking this as evidence."

"Evidence of what?" I asked.

"I'm not sure."

"Hey, Billy," I said as I looked around the burned out top floor, "if the fire started on the bed because Andrews was smoking, how come there is more damage in what used to be the kitchen?"

Where the walls and the ceiling were charred but more or less intact in the bedroom area, the kitchen was missing most of the outside walls and the burned out roof had collapsed.

"Sometimes fire spreads in random ways, but this is the first time I've had a chance to be up here, and I have to admit something seems to be wrong."

"How come?" asked Rob who had been following our conversation.

"One of my men asked if he could investigate this fire. He was eager to do it."

"Is that usual?" I asked. My experience tells me people don't volunteer for extra work unless they have an incentive.

"No it's not. I was a little surprised. I'll send a crew over this afternoon to do another investigation and I'll come myself."

"Do you think your man might have taken a bribe?" asked Rob. Bribes were common practice in city government, but not usually given to cover up a crime.

"Considering what the city pays us, I'm sure it's a possibility." Billy was looking very angry. I'd known Billy for several years and he was honest and hard working.

Rob continued to poke around in the ashes. He bent over and picked up something.

"What did you find?" I asked. He held out his hand, and I saw a bunch of amber glass that had cracked from the heat.

"This used to be a bottle, and if I'm not mistaken this bottle held laudanum."

"Laudanum? You mean an opium medicine? Isn't that used for pain?" I asked.

"And insomnia. It's a powerful sleeping potion."

"I am not happy," said Billy Bradshaw. "This could well be a crime scene and my department has been negligent in its investigation."

Rob looked around the room. "Either your men deliberately covered up a crime scene, or they were too lazy to really investigate. But I think this is now a police matter."

I loved it when Rob became the tough cop! I couldn't wait to get him home.

"Mail for you Mr. Jeremy," said Roscoe and he handed me a large envelope. As I suspected it was from Jenny Johnson. I sat at my desk and indicated that Roscoe should take his seat at his desk.

"It seems, Roscoe, that we are not done with the Cora Andrews case." I gave him the quick version of our visit to the burned out apartment.

"I'll get the file out," he said and went to the file cabinet. Meanwhile I opened the envelope and began reading.

Ina's second husband, Dr Richard Clarke, was an internist at Belleview Hospital after having moved to New York City. Ten years Ina's senior, he was a well-respected physician and well off financially. Jenny had given me the dates and facts, but she also had managed to interview some of his co-workers. Jenny had a way of making people comfortable, and they tell her things that they probably wouldn't usually confess.

According to what she had learned, Clarke was a kind man, but rather dull. Opinions about his wife Ina, however, were less guarded. Ina was disliked by almost everyone with whom Jenny spoke. People thought she was opinionated and officious.

When I met her she was charming and cordial. Of course now she was looking for a husband.

"Anything in that report of interest?" asked Roscoe.

"It seems that Ina picks husbands with bad hearts. Two of her husbands died of heart attacks."

"How about the third?"

"I haven't looked into that marriage yet, but I'll bet he also had a weak heart."

"It looks suspicious, doesn't it?"

"Indeed it does, Roscoe."

Velda was resplendent in a blue evening gown with rhinestones and a large floppy hat. Despite the heat, Velda looked cool and collected when I met her at the door.

"Cocktail?" I asked.

"Of course, darling. Where is the divine Detective Williams?"

"I'm right here," said Rob as he stepped into the hall with the cocktail shaker. Velda gave him a hug.

"We must spend more time together. You must come to Maine and get out of this beastly heat."

"Anytime," said Rob pouring out a drink and handing it to her.

"Where's Roscoe?" she asked. "I haven't seen him in a dog's age."

"I gave him the night off, and he took the car," I said. "How's the studio coming along?"

"It's all set up. I'm having my painting supplies shipped over there, and I'm off to Monhegan Island tomorrow."

"That's quite a trip," I added. I looked at my glass and saw it was already empty. I went over to the sideboard and made another.

"Nick Liberty offered to drive me to Port Clyde."

"Nick Liberty?" asked Rob. "As in Police Sergeant Liberty?"

143

"He said he knows you, Rob. You cops must all know each other."

"He works the waterfront if I'm not mistaken. How do you know him?"

"We met at an art gallery."

"Nick Liberty goes to art galleries?" I asked.

"Don't be such a snob, Jeremy. You and Rob aren't the only society misfits."

"Misfits?" Rob laughed.

"Well, you know what I mean."

"When are you coming back to Boston?" I asked.

"I'll be back in August before father arrives. Emma Goodwin's party should be fun."

"I'm not sure "fun" is how I'd describe it."

Jimmy Kirk announced dinner. We finished our drinks and headed into the dining room.

"This is festive," remarked Velda. I had to admit that Jimmy set a good table even for a small dinner party.

"Tell me more about this Nick Liberty," I said to Velda. "Are you dating him?"

"We've been on a few dates, yes."

"I can't see you with a cop," added Rob.

"The teapot is calling the kettle black," she said pointing at the both of us. "For your information he is a college graduate in anthropology and a minor in art history. He likes the adventure. and you both know that jobs are scarce. When the jobs come back he'll find something else."

"What about Tommy Beckford?" I asked. "Is that over?"

"I'm very fond of Tommy. I just don't want to be tied down just yet."

We finished the first course of chilled soup as Jimmy cleaned the table and brought us a nice chicken aspic with fruit salad. It was a perfect meal for a hot evening.

"I'll be so glad to get out of Boston with the heat coming," said Velda. "How are your cases going?"

"I'm working on an East Boston murder case," replied Rob. "It's pretty clear who is guilty, and I should have all the evidence in a day or two. I'm also working on the Dan Andrews murder case."

"Murder!" said Velda. "I thought he died in a fire."

"We have some evidence that the fire may have been staged and the original investigation was compromised," answered Rob.

"I thought it was *your* case?" Velda turned to me.

"It was in the beginning and now I guess it's *our* case."

"Speaking of which I saw Nora Wilde yesterday. How is that case coming along?" Velda went on to say they had a brief conversation about her father's upcoming wedding.

"Emma Goodwin took me calling with her, and we called on Ina Patterson. She wasn't at all like I thought she would be."

145

"Men!" sighed Velda as she shook her head. "You're all so easily deceived by a pretty face. You wouldn't recognize a murderess if you stumbled over one. Oh how lovely!" she exclaimed as Jimmy set a dish of orange sherbet in front of her.

Chapter 20

I slept fitfully during the night as the sea breeze died away and the air became heavy. The heat was becoming unbearable and even having fans wasn't helping. I got dressed and had an early breakfast. Rob had worked late and stayed at the apartment he kept in the Back Bay.

As early as it was the heat was just beginning to be uncomfortable and promised to break Boston's heat record. It was a short walk to Acorn Street to see my sister off. I rang the bell, and the door was opened by Nick Liberty. I had the impression that he may have spent the night.

"Hello," he said shaking my hand. "You must be Jeremy; I'm Nick." Nick was about six foot four with broad shoulders and very handsome in a blond Nordic way.

"Pleased to meet you. I came to see Velda off. I understand you're driving her to Port Clyde."

"I thought it would be fun to drive along the Maine coast and get away from the heat. I understand from the radio that it was unbearable in New York yesterday and that the heat is coming this way."

"I think it's already arrived."

"Jeremy, how wonderful to see you," said Velda as she came down the staircase. "Come in and have some coffee. Did you already have breakfast?" Velda was dressed in a red polka dot sun dress that showed a lot of leg.

"Yes, I did. Thank you."

"Velda has been telling me about some of your cases," said Nick. "And I've heard that you work with Detective Williams on occasion." He said it casually, but he gave me a knowing look. We headed into the dining room where Velda poured out a cup of coffee for me.

"We're working a case now as a matter of fact." I gave him the details of the Andrews death in the fire.

"It does sound suspicious," he agreed.

"I guess I'm destined to be surrounded with policemen and detectives," Velda sighed.

"You could do worse," I said.

"How long is the trip to Maine?" I asked.

"Going up route one should take about six hours," replied Nick.

"That's a long drive. You'll probably have to stay over," I said. Both Nick and Velda blushed a bit, which told me everything I needed to know.

"Do you have enough evidence to arrest them?" I asked.

Rob looked at me. "We know that we have a bottle of laudanum from the fire and a piece of jewelry that probably belongs to Cora Andrews. Cora Andrews had no reason to ever be in Mark Johnson's apartment."

"But that's circumstantial evidence."

"I know, but I'm bringing them in for questioning. Do you want to be present?"

"Yes, but how will you arrange that?"

"I'll bring you in as a special consultant."

"Let's get started," I said.

Detectives Benjamin White and Rob Williams brought Cora Andrews and Mark Johnson in for questioning. Both had been brought in separately and placed in different rooms with no time to communicate. I could see both interrogation rooms through the one-way glass in the observation room. Both were left in the room by themselves for over an hour and neither one looked comfortable.

"Cora Andrews was your client," said Rob to me. "Would you like to lead the questioning?"

"I certainly would," I answered. The three of us entered the room. Cora looked up at me and looked puzzled.

"You've met Detective Williams," I said. "This is Detective White. The police have retained me as a special consultant since this was my case originally."

"Why am I here?" she asked defensively.

"I'm sure you can figure that out," I answered. "Being an accessory to murder makes us very interested to hear what you have to say."

"What?" she asked and turned very pale and looked about to faint.

"Or," began Detective White, "you're the murderer and your boyfriend Johnson was the accessory."

"Murder," I reminded her, "carries the death penalty. If you cooperate with the police you may be able to avoid hanging." We had no solid evidence, and I just hoped Cora couldn't tell we were bluffing.

"It was Mark's idea," Cora said as sobs wracked her body. "I didn't know anything about it until afterwards."

"If that's true," said Rob, "that would make you an accessory after the fact which would be a lighter sentence."

"Let's get a stenographer in and get a statement," suggested White.

"You better tell us everything," I said. "And don't leave anything out."

I was pressing my luck by asking to be in on the interrogation of Mark Johnson. However, the police were used to me butting into police business and gave me a bit of leeway because I was a classmate of Rob Williams. At least that's how they thought of our relationship.

Mark Johnson sat on the steel chair in the interview room with his arms folded and a defiant look on his face.

"We just had an interesting talk with your girlfriend," I said as I sat down across the table from him. Rob and Benjamin took seats on either side of me.

"She's a liar."

"Is she?" I asked. "What is she lying about?" For just a moment he looked confused.

"If she said I killed him, she's a liar. It was her that did it."

"Killed? Dan Andrews was killed?" I countered. "I thought he died accidentally in the fire? We brought you in to talk about stealing the business documents and now you tell us Andrews was murdered?"

"That sounds like an admission to me," said Rob.

"Yes, it does," agreed Ben White. Mark Johnson looked panicked as he realized we had tricked him into confirming the murder of his cousin.

"What I don't understand," I said, "is why you murdered him. Cora's a nice looking woman, but she's nothing special. There are plenty of women out there. Doesn't seem like she's worth murdering your cousin for, but I guess love is blind."

"Love?" shouted Andrews. "I hate that woman! She's an evil bitch!"

"Evil? That sweet woman," I thought I'd play in that direction and see where it led. "According to her, she knew nothing of your plan until later, and then she was afraid that you'd hurt her if she went to the police."

"Hurt her? That woman is dangerous. She planned the whole thing. I didn't even know she killed him until a few days ago when she learned that you guys were investigating the fire."

151

"This is getting very interesting," said Rob as he rolled up his sleeves.

"Do you have an alibi for the time he was killed?"

"I was with Mary Marguerite Burk."

"Excuse me?" I said trying to hide my amazement.

"I said I was with Mary Marguerite. I met her a few weeks before the fire. The touring company was in Boston, and we hit it off. I admit to taking the papers, but when the fire broke out I was with her in New York."

"I thought," said Rob, "that you were with the Flowers woman."

"I met Viola after Mary Marguerite, and I broke it off."

"I hope for your sake," I said to Johnson, "that Mary Marguerite Burke will confirm your alibi."

"She hates me," replied Johnson. "I was the one who broke it off, and I doubt that she'll want to confirm my alibi."

"Don't worry about that," I answered. "Mary Marguerite owes me a favor. I found her a good lawyer and the least she can do is tell the truth." I looked at Mark Johnson to see if he was lying, but all I saw in his eyes was hope.

Chapter 21

Rob and I were gathered in the parlor before dinner. The windows were wide open and the fan was running and even inside the house the air was oppressive. Roscoe was mixing cocktails while we were filling him in on the latest developments of the Andrews murder.

"So it was the wife who set up the murder?" asked Roscoe. I indicated that he should sit down.

"It looks that way. Mark Johnson is an opportunist and a thief, but if he's not a murderer I don't want him going to jail for something he didn't do. We have enough on him already to send him up river," answered Rob as he sat back and sipped his martini.

"What bothers me," I added, "was the sloppy work of the original investigation. Something isn't right."

"Do you think the investigators were paid off?" asked Roscoe.

"That would explain the sloppy work," answered Rob. "I'm bringing them in tomorrow for questioning."

"A rubber hose might help loosen their tongues," suggested Roscoe.

"We never use rubber hoses," said Rob, not too convincingly.

"Of course not," I said as I rolled my eyes. "Mary Marguerite Burke is out on bail thanks to the good lawyer I got for her. I'm heading to New York tomorrow to talk to her and get a statement."

The door bell rang and Roscoe got up to answer it. Judy and Myra were joining us for dinner.

"Darlings, how wonderful to see you both," said Judy as she gave us each a peck on the cheek.

"Judy you look ravishing as usual," returned Rob. Judy had a long sleeveless black dress accented with a long string of pearls.

"And Myra," I added, "you look the consummate professional." She was dressed in a burgundy suit with a corsage of red and white roses.

"And you both look scrumptious in your white dinner jackets," returned Myra. "You put Hollywood to shame." Roscoe, who was at the sideboard mixing drinks, rolled his eyes.

"I saw that." I said to Roscoe.

"Must be the heat," he replied. "Ladies be blind."

"Speaking of the heat," broke in Rob, "the radio says it's only going to get hotter."

"Myra and I are heading to Bar Harbor soon. I can't stand the city when it's this hot.

"As soon as I can finish up my cases, Rob and I are heading up to the White Mountains."

"How are your cases going?" asked Myra.

"I'm still working on the Ina Patterson case, but we might have a break in another case if you'd like an exclusive."

"I'd kill for an exclusive. What have you got?"

Rob and I filled her in on the Andrews case, and I could swear that she was licking her chops in anticipation of a good story.

"As soon as I interview Mary Marguerite Burke and if she confirms Mark Johnson's alibi, then Rob will arrest the wife, Cora Andrews, for premeditated murder."

"Ladies and gentlemen," said Jimmy Kirk. "Dinner is served.

The first class car on the train to New York was no cooler than the third class car, I reflected as I watched the scenery pass by the window. It seemed to get hotter as the train got closer to the city. I'd have to change trains in New York and head up to Niagara Falls where Mary Marguerite Burke was out on bail. I was hoping that it would be cooler up north.

The death rate from the heat so far in late June was inching close to twelve thousand deaths. When I stepped off the train in New York the air was stifling, and I was afraid that I might become one of the statistics.

An hour later the train was pulling out of the city and to my relief the air was becoming somewhat cooler. I made my way to the dining car and had a tuna sandwich for lunch even though the heat had affected my appetite.

It was early evening when the train pulled into Niagara Falls. To my relief it was somewhat cooler here and the prospect of having to spend a few days here wasn't a problem.

The Falls View Hotel was crowded, and I when I asked if a room was available I was told that the hotel was completely booked. I took out a twenty dollar bill and passed it to the desk clerk.

"I believe I have a reservation."

The desk clerk looked at the bill, "Yes, sir. I see that you do." He reached over and rung the bell for the bell boy. "Please take Mr. Dance up to room 508."

"This way, sir," said the bell boy named Jimmy.

"Welcome back Mr. Dance. If there is anything else I can do for you, just let me know."

"Good to see you again, Jimmy," I said smiling. "Check in on me later if you'd like."

"I will," said Jimmy. "It will be my pleasure."

After breakfast in the hotel I headed over to the police station to see Ken McKenzie. I found him at his desk, and we shook hands.

"How can I help you, Jeremy?"

I told him about Mary Marguerite Burke and how she could provide some vital information in a murder case.

"She's staying in a motel on the outskirts of town. Would you like a lift out there?"

"I think it would be better if I go alone," I answered.

"Okay. It's a short walk." He gave me directions, and I was on my way.

As I got further away from the falls the neighborhood became less affluent. I found the rundown motel and knocked on the door of room twelve.

"Just a minute," yelled a voice from inside. "Who is it?"

"Mary Marguerite, it's me Jeremy Dance." The door flung open.

"Jeremy, come in. Sit down. I'd offer you a drink, but I don't have anything."

"Don't worry about it. I just need some information."

"Anything I can do, Jeremy. I can't tell you how grateful I am for you getting me a lawyer."

"I need to ask you about Mark Johnson."

"That scum?"

"Yes, that scum. He says he was with you when the fire broke out at his apartment. It would help if you told me the whole story."

"I never knew him as Mark Johnson. He told me at first his name was Mark Jones. We met after a show that the company put on in Boston. He took me out dancing that first night."

"Did you go back to his place at all?"

"No. He said he was from out of town and was staying at a boarding house in Cambridge."

"Was he?"

"Yes," she said and looked away. "I was staying there too."

I didn't ask about the sleeping arrangements, but I had a pretty good guess. "Were you with him when the fire happened?" I gave her the date and time of the fire.

"Yes, we were together all day that day. The next morning he read the paper at breakfast, said he had to do something, and then was gone."

"When did you see him again?"

"Not until we were in Niagara. Viola Flowers was yapping about her new boyfriend Dan Andrews. I saw them at a bar one night, and it was him. I knew he had played me. I tried to tell Viola that he was a liar, but she wouldn't believe me."

"Is that when…" I hesitated looking for the right word. "Is that when she had her accident?"

"Yes," she said. There were tears in her eyes and they were real.

"So you never knew him as Mark Johnson?"

"No."

"Okay then, I'm going to ask you and your lawyer to write out a statement that he was with you at the time of the fire. You're his only alibi."

"Does that mean he'll get out of jail?"

"Oh, no. He'll be in jail for a long, long time. All it means is that we can find the real killer of Dan Andrews. And just so you know, I think Johnson is scum, too."

She gave me a hug and thanked me again for helping her.

It was time to head back to Boston, but I thought I might delay a day or two and enjoy the break from the heat.

Rob came into my office with a self-satisfied grin on his face. I knew something was up but I wasn't going to let on.

"What's the matter?" I asked. "You look constipated."

"I had a little talk with the original fire investigation team." He was still grinning.

"A little talk? Was that with rubber hoses or brass knuckles?"

"You know the police don't use those."

"Sure they don't," I said. Of course everyone in Boston knew better.

"It seems Cora Andrews paid them off to do a quick job and find that Andrews was smoking in bed."

"I'm not surprised. Did you arrest them?"

"If I arrested every city employee who took a bribe, there wouldn't be anyone left."

"But this is a murder case."

"They didn't know that at the time. They just thought she was a relative looking for a quick insurance settlement."

"So you have enough to arrest her?"

"Yes, you want to come along?"

"The woman tried to use me, so yes I definitely want to come along." I picked up the phone and called Myra Pennington.

"Myra, darling, how would you like to be a witness to an arrest?"

Rob had commandeered my car, and I slipped into the passenger seat. Myra had rushed over as soon as I called and took the back seat. Cora Andrews was out on bail and since she lived in Cambridge, Rob had arranged for the local police to meet us at her house. They would have the honor of arresting her and transporting her across the river to Boston. The Cambridge police were waiting for us around the corner out of sight of the Andrews house. We parked out front of her house and the Cambridge police followed us up the sidewalk to the house.

I rang the bell and the maid answered the door. Her eyes opened wide when she saw us with two uniformed police officers standing behind us. Myra stayed in the background with a notepad and pencil.

"Where here to see Mrs. Andrews," said Rob.

"Mrs. Andrews is not receiving."

"This is not a social call," said Rob as he held up his badge. "Unless you want to be charged with obstructing justice you will get Mrs. Andrews here now."

"Come right in," she said and scurried off to find Cora.

"What's this all about and why are you terrifying my maid?" Cora Andrews demanded as she appeared in the hall.

"I have a warrant for your arrest for the death of your husband Dan Andrews," Rob said in a firm voice.

"Nonsense," she replied in a cool voice. "Mark Johnson killed my husband, and he threatened to kill me if I said anything."

"That's an interesting story, Cora," I said as I stepped forward. "But Mark Johnson says differently."

"He's a thief and a liar," she said, but was beginning to lose her confidence. "You can't believe him."

"You're right about that," said Rob. "But he has an alibi for the time of the fire, and we have witnesses that will testify that you bribed the fire investigators. These officers will escort you to headquarters to be booked for premeditated murder, so I suggest you come along quietly."

Cora knew she was defeated and allowed the officers to put her in handcuffs. The two police officers took Cora away in their police car.

"At least," I said as we stepped out into the heat, "the jail cell will be nice and cool for Cora."

"Sure," said Rob with a laugh, "she's one lucky broad."

"Myra, did you get what you need?" I asked.

"All I need now is to get to a telephone."

Chapter 22

Roscoe sat behind his desk in the office with a pencil in hand ready to take notes. Jimmy Kirk had left us with a pot of coffee and some sweet rolls.

"Roscoe," I said. "Finally I can concentrate on the Ina Patterson case. I'm not taking on any other cases for the summer, so please make my excuses if anyone asks."

"Yes, sir."

"If you'd like to take any of the cases, feel free. But I want to head out of the city as soon as I can."

"Too hot to work, reminds me of growing up in Mississippi. Not a lot of happy memories there."

"No wonder you moved to the frozen north."

"So where are we on the Ina Patterson case?" asked Roscoe.

"Not very far, I'm afraid. Nora Wilde will be getting quite frantic if I don't have something for her soon."

"What's your gut reaction, boss?"

"Well, three husbands died, which in itself is quite a coincidence. However, no one suggested that they weren't natural deaths. And we can't accuse her of anything if we have no evidence."

"You didn't answer my question, Mr. Jeremy."

"Okay. My gut tells me we need to look further. Here is what we have so far. Ina's first husband, Jacob Jensen, died of a heart attack at forty."

"Interesting," said Roscoe, who was taking notes.

"And you were the one who found out that Dr. Richard Clarke signed the death certificate and then became Ina's next husband."

"Indeed I did."

"And then Jenny checked out his reputation. Everyone liked him, but hated her. It's unlikely that he helped kill her first husband. He doesn't sound like the type."

"And he died of a heart attack?"

"Yes, but men have heart attacks in their forties."

"It's still rather odd, isn't it?" asked Roscoe.

"Of course, but we can't hang her for that."

"What about number three?"

"All I've got at this time is his name. It was Bruce Patterson. So our next step is to look into her third marriage."

"And if he died of a heart attack?"

"Then Ina Patterson is one bad luck woman. So pack a bag we're getting out of here."

"Where are we going?"

"We are going to Bar Harbor and enjoy the cool coast of Maine all because Bruce Patterson was thoughtful enough to die there."

For a moment I saw a look on Roscoe's face and knew what he was thinking. "Don't worry, Roscoe," I said trying to reassure him. "This is a resort for rich people. They've seen Negroes before. At the worst they'll just assume you're a servant." Every once in a while I get an impression of how different life must be for a man of color. It wasn't fair, and I hated it.

"If you say so, boss. Can I drive?"

"We'll share the driving, now go pack. I've got phone calls to make."

I called the Belmont Hotel and made reservations. Then I call Myra Pennington.

"Myra, I saw your story in the paper. It looks like the wire services picked it up."

"Jeremy, I can't thank you enough. This is the story of the decade. Love, deceit, fire, murder and the theft of bank documents, and then a tie-in to another murder. This story has it all."

"I wanted you to know that Roscoe and I are going to Bar Harbor. I need to follow up on Ina Patterson's third husband. We'll be staying at the Belmont. I know you and Judy are planning to go there."

"Yes, we're going at the end of the week. Is Rob coming with you?"

"Rob has to finish up a case for the police, and then he'll join me."

"I suppose you'll be driving?"

"Yes, I haven't had much opportunity to drive lately. And you?"

"We'll go by steamer. It's much more fun than the train."

"With any luck you may get another exclusive."

"That," she said, "will make my whole summer!"

The Belmont Hotel in Bar Harbor, Maine, had been a town fixture since 1879. My parents brought Velda and me to the Belmont every summer for the month of August. It was the one time of year when we were all together as a family. In the fall we were both sent off to school. During school vacations my father was always off somewhere making money.

I registered as Jeremy Van Clef since that was the name that the staff knew me by. Many of the staff had been here since I was a child.

"We have a room for you, Mr. Van Clef," The desk clerk smiled at me. It's good to see you again. We have a nice room for you and we've got a room in the staff wing for your valet."

"Thank you, Owen," I smiled. "But Mr. Jackson is my assistant, and you'll be kind enough to place him in an adjoining room." I shot Roscoe an "I told you so" look. I slipped Owen a ten dollar bill.

"I have two rooms on the second floor that I think you'll be comfortable in," said Owen as he opened the register book for me to sign.

After we unpacked I had coffee and sandwiches sent up to the room. My suite had a sitting room, a large bedroom and Roscoe's smaller room was across the hall.

"Sorry about the small room," I apologized.

"It's a palace compared to places I've stayed. You do realize that there are places where we couldn't even stay at the same hotel."

"People are stupid."

"No, sometimes they're just mean."

After lunch it was time to get to work. Bruce Patterson had been born in Bar Harbor. He grew up here and made a fortune in real estate, selling building lots to the rich. He also owned the local construction company who build the fine summer homes of the wealthy. He had met Ina when she spent a summer here after the death of her second husband. Some eighteen years her senior, he had married Ina at the end of the summer.

"What we need to do next is to look into the life of Bruce Patterson, because I have a feeling that there is more here that we need to know. Since he's only been dead for two years the information we get might be fresher."

"Where do we start?" asked Roscoe.

"Let's start with Island Real Estate, Bruce Patterson's company. It's still in business."

"Who owns it?"

"That's something we need to find out first."

Desk clerks, especially in small resort towns, usually know all the island gossip. My first stop was the front desk.

"Owen, I'm looking for island property. Who owns Patterson's Island Real Estate now that Bruce Patterson is dead?"

"His daughter Julie inherited the business."

"His daughter?"

"From his first marriage. His first wife died in childbirth."

"Thanks, Owen." I flashed him a smile and signaled Roscoe that we were leaving. "Let's go, Roscoe."

"Do you think we'll learn anything from the daughter?"

"Yes, Roscoe, I think Bruce Patterson's daughter will have a lot to say about her former step-mother."

Chapter 23

Island Real Estate and Construction had an office just outside of town. There were several trucks in the back lot, which seemed to mean that the construction business was doing well. It was a nice day, sunny with a cooling breeze and would be the perfect time to build a house.

The office, however, seemed to suggest success and understated wealth. My request to meet with Julie Patterson was granted even though I didn't have an appointment. We were ushered into a large, well furnished office. Julie Patterson was about thirty and wore glasses and a woman's dark red suit.

"How do you do, Miss Patterson," I said as we shook hands. "I'm Jeremy Dance and this is my assistant Roscoe Jackson."

"Pleased to meet you both. How may I help you?"

I explained my mission as best I could. I saw an interested look in her eyes when I got to the part about her former step-mother.

"You're checking into my father's death?"

"I'm checking into the deaths of all her husbands. It just seems strange that they all had bad hearts. If I may ask, how did your father die?"

"He died in a car crash. He was driving to work from his home and somehow he drove off the road and down a cliff into the bay."

"I see," I said. "So it really was an accident?"

"Yes, as much as I'd like to blame Ina for his death, she had nothing to do with it."

I could feel my case slipping away. So Ina's third husband didn't die of a heart attack. Maybe she wasn't a black widow after all. I could look into the death, but I wasn't sure I'd gain anything by it.

We said out goodbyes and Roscoe and I went back to the hotel.

"What now, boss?" asked Roscoe.

"I'll look into Bruce Patterson's death just to make sure, but then I think it's time to go home and tell Nora Wilde that we couldn't find anything suspicious about her future mother-in-law."

"So are we going home?" asked Roscoe.

"Oh, no. It's nice and cool here, and I've no desire to go back to the sizzling city just yet. Just to be sure, I want to check on this accident of Bruce Patterson. How about a walk over to the town library?"

"It's your dime, boss."

"You know you're not getting extra pay for this," I said.

"You be one mean cheapskate," replied Roscoe with a laugh.

The Jesup Memorial Library has a simple, understated red brick exterior that stands in stark contrast to the dark wood furnished interior. As a child I spent many happy hours at the library with my sister and our nurse. I think we read the entire

169

children's section in one summer. Happy memories flowed through my head as Roscoe and I entered the building.

With the help of one of the librarians we were able to search the archives for the news story about the death of Bruce Patterson. Roscoe read the news story to me.

Prominent Real Estate Developer Dies in Single Car Crash.

Bruce G. Patterson of Bar Harbor died in a car crash on Tuesday evening, according to the Hancock County Sheriff's Department. The single car crash was discovered the next day when Mr. Patterson failed to return home. A search for the missing man led investigators to discover the car which had failed to negotiate a sharp turn on the park loop road. The car was some thirty feet from the road and it appeared that the car had turned over several times throwing Mr. Patterson from the car.

The late Mr. Patterson was owner of Island Real Estate and Development. Mr. Patterson is survived by his daughter, Julie, of Northeast Harbor and his wife Ina Patterson. Mr. Patterson was predeceased by his first wife Angela Patterson. Services will be held at St. Savior's Episcopal Church on Saturday at noon.

"Maybe," I said, "I should pay a visit to the sheriff's office."

"Do you think there's something wrong?"

"It just seems too convenient. If Ina Patterson is the unluckiest wife in the world, she seems to benefit with the death of each husband."

"And," added Roscoe," they were all rich."

Buck Belrose sat behind his sheriff's desk as Roscoe and I entered. He gave us the quick once over and his eyes lingered a few seconds longer on Roscoe. We were both used to it by now. Other than the movies, few people of the extreme north had ever seen a person of color up close.

"What can I do for you boys?" he asked. I could feel Roscoe bristle beside me. Buck Belrose was in his late fifties, so in comparison I guess we were boys. It was a typical Maine greeting, and not meant to be offensive. I'd have to explain that to Roscoe later.

"I'm Jeremy Dance and this is Mr. Jackson," I said with emphasis, "my assistant. We're looking into the death of Bruce Patterson." I passed him my business card.

"I see," said the sheriff. "What do you want to know?"

"You were the one who worked the accident. I'd like your take on it."

"It was no accident, I can tell you that."

"What?"

"I think you two had better sit down," he said and pointed to the two stiff-backed chairs. Roscoe had his notebook out and ready to take notes.

"What makes you think it wasn't an accident?"

"Bruce Patterson grew up on the island. He knew every inch of the roads here. There is no way he would have driven off the Island Loop Road."

"Then why was it recorded as accidental death?"

"There was no solid evidence that it was anything else. But I've known Bruce for years, and I'm telling you he didn't drive off the road."

"I see," I said.

"And there was one other thing that the papers didn't report," said the sheriff. "When we found the car the gear shift was in neutral."

"So?" I wasn't quite sure what that meant.

"So you don't drive a car in neutral, do you? The car won't go anywhere if you do."

"Maybe he shifted into neutral to stop and look at the scenery."

"In that case the car would have just rolled off the road and stopped. No, the car was going at some speed to end up where it did. The car was shifted into neutral at the top of the hill and rolled over the edge of the road."

"And?" I asked.

"And that means one of two things. He either committed suicide or he was pushed."

"Murder?" asked Roscoe.

"Oh, yes," said the sheriff, "I believe it was murder."

What he told me next gave me more reasons to be suspicious.

"He called me 'boy'," said Roscoe accusingly as we left the office. Roscoe was used to me defending him in those situations.

"He didn't call you 'boy'; he called both of us 'boys.' It's the way they talk here," I said.

"Hmmm."

"And the real point here is that the sheriff thinks he was murdered."

"But he couldn't prove it?"

"No, he couldn't. And apparently the widow claimed that he had been depressed for days and talked of suicide."

"You think he committed suicide?" asked Roscoe.

"I'm inclined to go with the sheriff's view. Buck Belrose knew Bruce Patterson, and only Ina says Bruce was depressed."

"So what we have here…"

"What we have here," I said interrupting Roscoe, "is another convenient death for Ina Patterson."

"How many suitcases did you bring?" I asked staring at the pile of suitcases and boxes piled on the steamboat wharf.

"Just a few things," said Judy Hogarth as she watched Roscoe try to fit everything in the car and still leave room for the four of us to ride.

"Only one of those is mine," said Myra Pennington.

"Why am I not surprised?" I asked.

"Well, it was nice of you to pick us up," cooed Judy.

"I wouldn't think the hotel would appreciate picking up this much luggage," I answered.

"All set," said Roscoe. Somehow he had managed to fit everything into the car.

"I hope you're going to keep those jewels in the hotel safe," I said pointing to Judy's long string of pearls.

"I'll be wearing them most of the time," she said as we all got into the car.

"My, it's much more pleasant here than in Boston," remarked Myra as we headed up to the hotel.

"Still hot there is it?" I asked.

"Brutal," answered Judy. "Where's Velda?"

"She's at her new studio on Monhegan."

"Is what's-his-name with her?"

"No, she has a new beau."

"What's his name?"

"Nick Liberty, he is a policeman."

"That's interesting," said Myra. "The twins both have policeman boyfriends."

"When is Rob coming?" asked Judy.

"He should be here on Friday,"

"We're here, folks," said Roscoe as we pulled up to the Belmont.

Chapter 24

It was late afternoon when the steamer came into port. I spotted Rob waving from the top deck as the ship docked. Judy, Myra, and I waited while the passengers filed out onto the wharf.

"Planning to stay awhile?" I asked. Rob had two suitcases, one in each hand.

"As long as I can. Boston is burning up in the heat."

"The weather's been great here," I said.

"You're looking healthy," said Myra with an admiring glance in his direction.

"Rob always looks healthy," added Judy. "Men are so lucky. They don't need makeup to make them look presentable."

"Neither of you need makeup," replied Rob. I loaded up the car and the four of us headed to the Belmont.

"This really is a nice hotel," said Judy as we pulled up to the Belmont. "My family came to Bar Harbor on vacations. But we stayed at the hotel down the road."

"I'm sure that was as good," I said. "Rob, why don't you go unpack and we'll all meet at the bar for a drink."

"Perfect," agreed Rob.

"How's the investigation going?" asked Rob when he and I were seated at the bar.

I told him about my visit to the sheriff and his suspicions that Bruce Pennington's death was not an accident.

"But no solid proof?" asked Rob.

"No. None at all. Yet."

"Well, here is an interesting piece of news. The old lady who was living with Ina Patterson died suddenly."

"What?"

"I was in the newspaper. It seems that Miss Mildred Blasdell had tons of money and was a society leader. They just casually mentioned that she was staying with Ina Patterson."

"There you two are!" exclaimed Myra. "What evil are you two cooking up?" Judy and Myra had somehow managed to change into tennis clothes.

"Wouldn't you like to know," teased Rob.

"Want to join us for tennis?" asked Judy.

"You know we can beat you," I said.

"Care to place a bet?" asked Judy.

"You're on," said Rob with a wink. "You girls run along and practice while we go change."

"They're going to beat us," I said as soon as Judy and Myra left.

"Of course they are," replied Rob. "We have other activities we excel at."

"Yes," I said catching his meaning, "we do at that."

We never got to finish the match. About half way through the game we heard a voice calling us.

177

"Hey, anyone want to buy a girl a drink?" It was Velda. She was wearing a billowing summer dress with a matching floppy hat.

"What are you doing here?" I asked.

"When I got your letter that you were coming here for a few days I decided that I didn't want to miss the party."

"What about your painting?" asked Judy.

"Monhegan is boring compared to Bar Harbor. I can paint here as well as there. This place reminds me of those long lazy summers we spent here as kids."

"That's what I felt," I agreed. "Are you staying here at the Belmont?"

"Oh yes. Just like old times. Now how about that drink?"

The bar at the Belmont had been a library during prohibition. The room was oak paneled and retained the bookshelves filled with leather-bound volumes. The old kerosene light fixtures had been electrified, but other than that it looked exactly the way I remembered it from childhood.

"Why are you really here?" asked Velda. We were seated at a table in the corner. Each of us was nursing a cocktail. "I'm guessing my brother is on a case and you, Myra, are onto a story. Judy, you're here to be with Myra, and Rob is here to do unspeakable things with my brother."

"The Patterson case led me here," I answered. "Not to mention the weather is much cooler."

"And I'm always interested in a big story," agreed Myra.

"And I have a feeling that whatever Jeremy uncovers is going to be a police matter," said Rob. "And of course I'm here to do unspeakable things with your brother."

"Ina Patterson lived here in Bar Harbor with her third husband. He died and left her lots of money," I stopped for a moment to sip my drink before continuing. "Roscoe and I did a little research and found out that he was killed in a car accident. So she lost two husbands to bad hearts and one to an automobile accident."

"Well," said Velda, "You can't blame her for an accident."

"Except," I said, "that the sheriff said the car was shifted into neutral."

"So?" asked Velda.

"You don't drive a moving car in neutral. The sheriff suspects foul play, and I tend to agree with him."

"Murder?" asked Velda.

"There's no other evidence. Ina claimed at the time that he had been depressed, so the authorities ruled it a possible suicide. They hushed it up publically because he was a community leader."

"You don't believe it was suicide, do you?" asked Judy.

"I do not," I said.

The morning breeze came through the open window and the sun was shining in my eyes. I looked at the clock and saw it was already nine in the morning. Rob was already up and in the bathroom. I could smell something in the air.

"I smell smoke," I said as Rob stepped into the bedroom.

"I smelled it earlier. There must be a fire somewhere."

I got up and went to the window. "Look over there in the distance. You can see a column of smoke."

"Someone's camp fire probably got out of control."

"No. that's over at the edge of the village."

"We'll have to check it out later," I said. "Let's get some breakfast."

Judy and Myra had already left for a day of hiking, so it was just Roscoe, Velda, Rob, and me for breakfast in the dining room.

"What are you going to do today?" I asked Velda.

"I'm going to Acadia and paint. I think one of those divine carriage trails with a stone bridge would make a great painting. What are you three planning?"

"I think we'll take another trip to see Sheriff Buck Belrose," I answered.

"How come?" asked Roscoe.

"I think he has more information than he's telling us. There was something about his body language that makes me think so."

"Body language?" asked Velda.

"I read some studies done by psychiatrists at Mass General in the twenties that suggest that people often express themselves non-verbally without realizing it. For instance, you've looked at your watch twice so far, which leads me to believe you are anxious to get going on your day."

"Yes, that's true. I really can't wait to go out and paint." The waitress came and took our plates away and refilled our coffee. Velda excused herself and headed out.

"You boys back again?" asked the sheriff. "What can I do for you now?"

Rob introduced himself as a Boston detective. "So I've got one police detective, one private investigator and one assistant investigator. I could use some help here."

"Help?" I asked.

"We don't see a lot of serious crime here," continued the sheriff. "Mostly car accidents and a few drunks. You guys see the fire this morning?"

"Yes," Rob answered.

"It was set. It's the third fire this summer. I don't have any leads."

"Do they have anything in common?" I asked.

"Yes, indeed. They all belong to Patterson's Island Real Estate."

"Well, that was an interesting piece of news," I said as the three of us headed into a local diner for coffee. The old storefront has a small counter with about a dozen stools. Behind the counter was an array of burners and grills and a huge coffee pot. We were served by middle age waitress in a white apron.

"The fires?" asked Roscoe.

"Yes, but he wasn't very helpful about Bruce Patterson's accident," said Rob.

"I still think he's holding back something," I added.

"What do we do now?" asked Roscoe.

"I think it's time to pay another call on Julie Patterson."

Chapter 25

The news out of the Midwest wasn't good, to say the least. The heat wave showed no signs of letting up. Both New York and Boston were sweltering, and I had no desire to return to the city anytime soon. I knew Rob would have to return soon, and he wasn't too anxious to go either.

I had sent an update to Nora Wilde detailing my investigation into Ina Patterson. She wasn't surprised by anything I uncovered, but she did remind me that her father's wedding to Ina was coming up soon.

"Can you put in for a leave of absence?" I asked Rob.

"I can put in for it, but I won't get it. Do you know what happens to the crime rate when the city heats up?"

"I have a pretty good idea."

"So let's enjoy the next few days."

"Agreed," I answered.

Julie Patterson was seated behind her desk when Rob and I walked in. She looked up. "Don't tell me you've decided to buy a nice summer place here in Bar Harbor?"

"That's not a bad idea," said Rob as we both took a seat.

"I came to discuss your father," I said.

"I figured as much," she said with a sigh. "Can't you just let it go?"

183

"No, I can't. The sheriff thinks there was something suspicious about Bruce's death."

"Like what?"

"Like the fact that the car was shifted into neutral."

"I don't understand."

"People don't drive cars on winding roads in neutral."

"Maybe he was coasting."

"Maybe, but not likely. And your step mother claimed that he had been depressed. She hinted at suicide, but tried to keep it out of the papers."

"What?" Julie looked pale.

"Where were you when this happened?" asked Rob, shifting into his cop persona.

"I was away in California."

"Is it possible that he committed suicide?" asked Rob.

"No, it is not!" she almost shouted. "Ina's a liar if she said that."

"Okay," I said. "There's something I'd like you to consider if you feel that way."

"What?"

"I'd like you and the sheriff to get together and go to the authorities."

"What for?"

"To have your father exhumed," I replied. For a moment I thought she might faint, but then some color returned to her face.

"Can I do that? Can't Ina object?"

"Well," said Rob, "I'm no lawyer, but I think there may be ways around it. I assume since your father left the business to you that you are his heir. Correct?"

"Yes, that's true. Ina was left some money, but I am the executrix and have control of his estate."

"I'm pretty sure his estate includes his body, especially if the funeral arrangements were left for you," continued, Rob. "And just to be sure, let's say that you don't like where he is buried. Maybe you want to have him moved. And let's say you want the coroner to take another look."

"What are we looking for?" she asked.

"Traces of drugs that may have had an effect on your father. Maybe he fell asleep or was drugged, or maybe he was poisoned," I said.

"And you think that bitch could have done that?"

"It's just a theory," added Rob.

"So really," Julie said looking at me, "this helps out your case. What does this do for me? My father will be just as dead."

"You'll help put the woman away who did this," I said. "And prevent her from killing anyone else."

"If she did it," Rob reminded her.

"The thought of Ina rotting away in jail is a pleasant thought. On one condition," she said looking at us both. "You're both detectives, correct?"

"Yes," said Rob.

"I'll have my father exhumed on the condition that you find out who the hell is burning down my properties."

It was tea time, and we all gathered at a table to enjoy our afternoon ice tea. I detest hot tea, but love ice tea. By now everyone at the hotel was used to seeing Roscoe and had stopped staring at us whenever we entered a public place.

Judy and Myra were still in their tennis outfits, but Velda was resplendent in a new green cocktail dress with sequins. Rob and I had put on ties, but we were forgoing suit jackets in deference to the summer heat. Roscoe was neat as always with his starched white shirt and bow tie. Roscoe poured our tea, more out of habit than expectation.

"I forgot to ask you about Nick Liberty," I said to Velda.

"He had to go back to Boston to work."

"Is it serious?" asked Judy.

"Serious enough."

"What do you know about his background?" asked Rob.

"Now, don't you two be snobs about this," she said looking at Rob and me. "For your information he comes from a very respectable family. He has a college degree and just like someone else at this table I could name, he likes being a policeman."

"He is very good looking," said Rob in a teasing tone.

"And has a well-built body, too," I added licking my lips.

"You two stay away from him," she said laughing but looking alarmed at the same time. "After you two corrupted poor Jimmy Donovan, he wasn't much use to me."

"Jimmy Donovan," I said, "didn't need much corruption, as you call it."

"He seemed to know pretty much what he was doing," agreed Rob.

"Stop it you two," Velda moaned and took another tea cake off the plate.

"What did you two do today," asked Myra to change the subject.

We gave a brief account of the day's events.

"Arson?" asked Myra. "There's another story for me. I want an exclusive. The papers eat up this type of stuff."

"Well," said Rob. "It's only a story if we can find out who is doing it."

Chapter 26

Rob was due to leave tomorrow for Boston, and on our last day together we were looking at the hull of a burned out building. It was difficult to picture what type of building had been here before the fire.

"I hate that smell," I said looking around at the ruins of a half-built house. All that was left was the charred remains of the back wall, the rest being reduced to rubble.

"Not much left," I said. "I don't know how the fire department knows it is arson."

"I'm guessing that the gas can over there," said Rob pointing to a pile of refuse under the tree, "is what we call a clue."

"Smart ass."

"Thanks. I think we should look around."

I wandered around the lot. By the size of the basement wall, this was going to be a big house. In the back of the lot I stopped and looked closely at something on the ground.

"Hey, Rob, over here."

"What did you find?"

"These," I said as I picked up two empty beer bottles.

"If these are related to the fire, then we're looking for two people, not just one."

"I think we should go talk to the firemen. They're more likely to talk to you as a police detective than to me a simple private investigator."

"No one," said Rob, "could ever call you simple."

Brian Champion seemed to be too young to be fire chief as he greeted us. About six feet tall with flaming red hair, I placed him at about our age. His friendly greeting put us at ease as we sat in his small office.

"I understand that Julie Patterson hired you to look into the fires that are burning down her buildings."

"News travels fast," I said.

"This is a small town," Brian replied. "There are no secrets."

"What can you tell us about the fires?" asked Rob.

"There have been three fires deliberately set in the last month. The first was a commercial building that Julie was building for the Island Coal Company. The second one was a stable for one of the summer folks. And yesterday's fire was a house Julie was building on speculation. All three were doused in gasoline and set afire."

"Do you think they're targeting Julie or just new construction?" I asked.

"There have been six or seven new constructions going up on the island, and only Julie's projects have been burned down," replied Brian.

"I see," said Rob. "Have you by chance noticed anyone at the fires watching?"

"As I said, it's a small town. Everyone shows up to watch a fire."

"Do you have any suspects in mind?" I asked.

"At first I thought it might be some island kids doing it. But I think if it were, the fires would be more random. I think Julie is the target."

"I think I'd agree with that," said Rob.

"Thank you for your time," I said getting up from the chair.

"Let me know if I can help any further," said Brian as we all shook hands.

"Seems like a nice guy," said Rob on our way back to the hotel.

"You have a thing for red heads?"

"No, I have a thing for rich handsome men who ask annoying questions," laughed Rob.

Roscoe was busy back at the hotel typing up the notes I'd been handing him all week. He looked up as we entered the suite. "What did you learn?"

"Well," I began, "we know that the only fires set were on Julie Patterson's property, and that it's possible that there are two of them and that they drink beer."

"What type of beer?" Roscoe asked.

"That's a good point," I said. "I have no idea."

"Labatts," replied Rob. "You need to pay attention."

"What's Labatts?" asked Roscoe.

"It's a Canadian beer. We are less than one hundred miles from the border."

"I didn't know you knew beer," I remarked to Rob.

"I know lots of things."

"I'll bet," I said under my breath.

"If we can find out where in town they sell it, we might be able to find the fire-starter," observed Roscoe.

Velda showed up at dinner with a very cleaned up and well-dressed Nick Liberty. Myra and Judy had decided to have dinner in town, and Roscoe was taking dinner in his room. I suspected he was still somewhat ill at ease in the all white dining room.

"Good evening, Nick," I said. "I didn't know you were coming."

"It was a surprise," said Velda quickly, though I suspected otherwise.

"Time off for good behavior, Mr. Dance."

"Please call me Jeremy."

"How is Boston?" asked Rob. "I'm heading back tomorrow."

"Very hot and the inhabitants of the city are getting very restless," Detective Williams.

"Call me Rob. We aren't on duty."

"So are you staying at the hotel?" I asked innocently. I was pleased to see that they both turned a bright shade of red.

"Where's the waiter?" asked Rob, rescuing the moment.

191

"I could use a drink first," said Velda recovering.

During a round of cocktails I explained what we had learned about the arson fires in Bar Harbor, which wasn't much.

"I'll be here for a couple of days. I'd be happy to help," offered Nick.

"I'd loved some help," I said flashing a smile. My sister shot me a warning look.

Just then the waiter came to take our food order. Surprisingly we all ordered baked stuffed lobster. Though I much preferred steamed lobster in the shell, it's not the type of food for a formal dining room.

"So how long are you staying here?" asked Velda.

"As soon as I find out more information of Ina Patterson's last husband, and hopefully find the arsonist, then I'll head back to Boston."

"How did you get the arson case?" asked Nick.

"Blackmail," I sighed. "Julie Patterson said she'd have her father exhumed if I found out who was setting the fires."

"Exhumed?" asked Nick.

"Her father died in a car accident that seems somewhat suspicious. I want to know if he was poisoned or drugged."

"You think Ina killed him?" asked Velda.

"It's a possibility," I said as the first course of clam chowder arrived.

Rob and I were up early for breakfast. I helped him pack, and then I saw him off at the dock. He was taking a steamer to Portland and then catching the train for Boston. I watched the steamer disappear and suddenly wished I was going with him.

"What are we going to do now, Mr. Jeremy?" asked Roscoe when I returned to the car.

"We are going to wake up Mr. Liberty and track down some beer bottles."

Chapter 27

I was sitting on the front porch of the hotel having my second cup of coffee when Nick Liberty appeared. He was dressed in a freshly pressed white shirt with the sleeves rolled up and wearing a wide brimmed hat. Striking was too mild a word for the figure he cut.

"Where's my lazy sister?" I asked.

"Still sleeping. She told me to get lost today because she's going out painting, so I'm at your disposal."

"First I think we need to pay another visit to Julie Patterson. We need to figure out why she's the fire bug's target."

"What's your theory?"

"It's got to be either personal or business. I don't think anyone gains financially from the fires."

"I agree. Let me get a cup of coffee and we'll go. Is Roscoe coming?"

"I'm trying to give Roscoe some time off while we're here. He works double duty at home running my household and being my assistant. I'm sending him home soon."

"Does he feel out of place here?"

"He doesn't say so, but I think he's more comfortable in Boston. Here he's kind of a novelty."

We sat and talked for another twenty minutes sipping our coffees before we started out.

"This is your car? Wow! A Cadillac 452-D."

"Yes, and you can bet that Roscoe offers to drive me anytime I need to go somewhere."

"I don't blame him."

"Would you like to drive?" I asked.

"Does a bear shit in the woods?"

Nick got behind the wheel with a big grin on his face, started the car, and shifted it into first gear. "Smooth," he said as we took off down the road.

Julie Patterson wasn't in her office, and we were told she was out on a construction site in Northwest Harbor. Nick was happy to drive the extra distance.

A hand painted sign told us we had arrived at the construction site of Patterson's Island Real Estate and Construction. Julie was dressed in men's overalls and flannel work shirt.

"Nice outfit," I said as we approached her while she was examining a set of blueprints.

"Does this look like a garden party to you?" she asked. She looked at Nick with more than just curiosity. "And you are?"

"This is Sergeant Nick Liberty of the Boston Police," I said by way of introduction.

"Do you always hang out with tall, handsome cops?"

"As often as possible," I answered.

"Did you find the arsonist yet?"

"I've got a few leads," I answered being vague. "I do have a few questions to ask you."

"Okay, let's go sit down somewhere." We looked around but the only place to sit was a pile of lumber by the stone foundation. We made the best of it.

"You seen to be the target," said Nick shifting into his police sergeant role. "Do you have any enemies?"

"Not really, no. There is another rival construction company on the island, but there's more than enough work to go around, even if there is a depression."

"Who is it?" I asked.

"Buddy Levesque. He does mostly repairs and additions, and maybe a small cottage or two. So we're not even really in competition."

"Where can I find this Buddy Levesque?" I asked.

"Last I knew he was working on a house over in Bass Harbor."

"Any former boyfriends we should be looking at?" asked Nick.

"Half the men on the island are ex-boyfriends," she laughed giving Nick a look that conveyed more than a little interest.

"Anyone we should be giving a closer look at?" I asked.

"Let me think about it," she said as she stood up from her seat on the wood pile. "I really need to get back to work."

"If you think of anything," I said as we headed toward the car, "contact me. I'm at the Belmont."

"Oh, by the way," she said just as I was about to get in the car, "I got the exhumation order signed. The body will be exhumed in a few days."

"Slow down!" I yelled as Nick opened the throttle on the island road. "You'll send us over the cliff."

"We're nowhere near a cliff," replied Nick. "You should see me in a police car."

Bass Harbor was a typical island town. It wasn't hard to find the house that Buddy Levesque was working on. We pulled into the driveway that held a new Ford V8 pickup truck.

"Are you Buddy Levesque?" I asked getting out of the passenger seat. Buddy was close to fifty and balding.

"Yes. Who wants to know?" Buddy looked at us with suspicion.

"I'm Jeremy Dance and this is Sergeant Liberty," I said. I didn't bother to explain that we weren't with the local police.

"What can I do for you?"

"We're looking into the arson fires."

"Terrible business. What do you want with me?"

"We'd just like to ask you a few questions."

"Go ahead."

"Were you aware that all the fires that were set were on property of Julie Patterson?"

"No," he said thinking it over. "I never gave it much thought."

"I understand that you and Julie were rivals," said Nick in his best cop voice.

"Who told you that?" asked Buddy laughing. "We're not even in the same business. I do repairs and small construction. I work alone and Julie has a whole crew. In fact Julie sometimes hires me to work on houses before she sells them. If you think I had anything to do with the fires, you're crazy."

"No one is accusing you, Mr. Levesque," I said. "We were just wondering if you know of anyone who might have something against Julie Paterson."

"No I don't. Julie runs an honest business. This is a small place, Mr. Dance. Everyone knows everyone else."

"Thank you for your time, Mr. Levesque. Let's go Nick."

Back on the car I turned to Nick. "Do you believe him?"

"It's hard to say. My police sense tells me he's telling the truth."

"I can't tell." I said. "I think we better track down some Labatt's beer."

"To drink?"

"That, too."

By the time Nick and I asked at the fourth store, it was becoming apparent that Labatts beer wasn't readily available on the island. No store that we could find carried it. That meant that whoever left the empty bottles at the fire must have gotten them off the island. There were two likely scenarios. Either they bought then in another town or a fishing boat brought them from Canada. The fishermen wouldn't be in until evening, so Nick and I headed to Ellsworth the largest town near the island. This time I drove.

A search along Ellsworth's Main Street didn't turn up any place that sold Labatts beer. It was time for lunch so we headed into a small diner and took seats at the lunch counter. We ordered a sandwich and coffee from the guy behind the counter. He was wearing a gray shirt with the name Bob embroidered on the pocket.

"Do you know," asked Nick as the sandwich plate was placed in front of him, "where we might get some Labatts beer?"

"The only place I know where you might get it is over at the general store in Hancock. They get a shipment in once in a while. Used to be lots of Labatts drinkers during prohibition. Now of course American beer is much cheaper," offered Bob.

"How do we get to Hancock?" I asked. Maine had so many small towns scattered about and I had no idea where Hancock was.

"Just stay on route one northeast. Can't miss it."

"Thanks," I said.

It took us about forty-five minutes of turning, twisting road before we arrived in Hancock. The general store was easy enough to find. The town was small with a town hall, school, and a railway station in the center.

The general store seemed to sell a little bit of everything. We walked in and were greeted by a sixtyish woman with gray hair wrapped up in a bun. She was wearing a flowered apron.

"What can I do for you gentlemen?" she asked.

"We were hoping you sell Labatts beer?" I said.

"I've got a couple left in the icebox. I can sell it to you, but I can't serve it. Laws, don't you know. But if you were to take them out back of the store and drink them, well who's to say."

I looked at Nick and he nodded. I took out my wallet and paid for them, and we headed out the back of the store where we found a picnic table under a tree. "Looks like this gets a lot of use," I said looking around.

"Pretty good set up," agreed Nick.

"This is nice. We could be back in Boston in the sweltering heat."

We finished our beer and went back into the store. The old lady looked up from her bookkeeping as we reentered the store.

"Do you sell a lot of this brand of beer?" asked Nick.

"Can't say that we do," she answered with a wary look. "Why are you asking?"

"Well," I began. I thought it was better to be honest at this point. "We're looking into the arson fires over in Bar Harbor. Labatts beer bottles were found on the scene of the fire."

"I knew those two were up to no good. Giving themselves airs with their expensive beer."

"What two?" I asked.

"The Jenkins boys. They've been in trouble since they could walk. I wouldn't put it past them to set fires."

"Who are these Jenkins boys?" asked Nick.

"Two brothers over in Southwest Harbor. James and Matthew. Good biblical names, but trust me there's nothing religious about either one of those two."

"Thanks," I said. "You've been very helpful."

Back in the car we rode for a while before one of us spoke. "We can't really prove that they set the fires you know," said Nick. "Even if the beer bottles were theirs, that doesn't mean that they set the fires."

"Proof is for law courts," I said. "I don't care about proof. I don't need proof. A little fear of retribution is all the justice I need to give out."

"What are you going to do?"

"I'm going to satisfy myself that they are responsible, and then we're going to pay them a visit."

Chapter 28

It was an overcast day and the sea breeze kept the island cool. I couldn't help but feel sorry for the poor people who were suffering in the heat wave that had taken over the country. It was so hot and unrelenting that several radio preachers were predicting the end of days.

Julie Patterson and some onlookers were gathered at the cemetery as the sheriff was supervising the disinterment of Bruce Patterson's remains. There were about a dozen of us watching as three men dug up the grave and piled a mound of dirt to one side of the hole.

I worried about Julie as she watched them uncover the top of the coffin. She looked grim, but didn't seem to be in any danger of fainting. Velda had come along for moral support and was standing with Julie.

"You really don't need to be here," I said to her. "This is a legal proceeding and the sheriff has it under control."

"I know," she said. "I just hate to leave him."

There was a tent set up beside the grave where they intended to do the autopsy, or whatever it was called at this point. There were now five men attempting to open the coffin. I took Julie by the arm and led her away. She didn't resist. I led her to my car and Roscoe opened the door for her to sit down in the back seat. I got in beside her. Velda got into the back seat from the other side of the car so that Julie was seated between us.

"Do you know James and Matthew Jenkins?" I asked.

"Yes, why?"

"I suspect they may be involved in setting fire to your property." I looked over at the grave site and noticed that they were moving something into the tent. "How do you know them?"

"I was engaged to Matthew."

"Who broke it off?" I asked.

"I did."

"Why?"

"Because he was drunk and he hit me."

"Is that normal behavior for him" I asked.

"I didn't think so, but I began to see little things that sent up a warning, so I ended it with him."

"How did he take it?"

"He was angry, furious actually. We haven't spoken since. You think he set the fires?"

"I think so. What about the brother?"

"James is the older brother, and I wouldn't put it past him. He's a mean one. Are you going to the sheriff?"

"I'll talk to the sheriff, but he won't be able to do anything unless we have evidence. But don't worry. I plan to take care of it."

Nick stepped out of the tent and was waving to me. I told Julie to stay in the car with Velda and went over to where Nick was standing.

"What's up?" I asked.

"The coroner is taking some samples and making some notes. I think you need to hear this."

Inside the tent the mortal remains of Bruce Patterson was spread out on a makeshift table. I hadn't seen that many dead bodies and this is the first exhumation I had ever seen. The body was remarkably well-preserved I thought. The flesh had shrunken and looked like a skin covered skeleton, which on reflection I guess is exactly what it was. The clothing was still in good condition. I guess there are some things you can take with you.

"Tell Mr. Dance here what you suspect," said Nick to the doctor.

"I can't be certain until I do more tests, but there inconsistencies here that make me think this gentleman was poisoned."

"Why wasn't it discovered before?" I asked.

"It was an accident. There was little reason to look further and the signs of poisoning are easy to miss if you are not looking for them," stated the doctor.

"This changes everything," I said. "And Ina Patterson becomes suspect number one."

"Telegram for you Mr. Van Clef," said the desk clerk when we returned to the hotel. It still startled me when I was addressed by that name. I had told him earlier that any correspondence to Mr. Dance should be directed to me, explaining that it was my professional name.

"Thank you," I said and took the cable and sat in the lobby to read it. The letter was from Nora Wild and briefly stated that Ina and her father had moved up their wedding plans. No doubt it was Ina's idea. This meant that I had to speed up my investigation. I took a walk to the telegraph office and sent two telegrams. One to Nora and one to Rob.

"You're going to do what?" asked Julie Patterson from behind her desk in the Patterson office.

"I'm going to set a trap for the Jenkins brothers. I just need you to go along with it."

"You think it will work?"

"Maybe, maybe not. It's worth a try. If I can't catch them in the act, I'll make a little visit they won't soon forget. But I'd rather see them off to jail. You know Doris Butler, don't you?"

"Yes, she's a friend of mine."

"And she writes the gossip column for *The Acadian*."

"Yes, she does."

"Then you need to come with me while we call on Doris," I said.

Doris Butler was the same age as Julie, but dressed much more flamboyantly. She had a bubbly personality that I think could become very tiresome after a time.

"I'd be happy to help," Doris said after we explained what we wanted her to do. "I have an afternoon deadline and the paper will come out on Friday. I'm short of material anyway."

205

"If this works there will be a good news story for you," I said.

"I don't really write news stories," said Doris with a wistful sigh.

"I have a friend who was a society columnist, and she went on to become a national reporter. I think you should meet her. Her name is Myra Pennington."

"Myra Pennington? Why I've heard of her. She's even interviewed Mrs. Roosevelt."

"Join us for dinner tonight at the Belmont. You too, Julie."

"Oh, I'd love to meet her," gushed Doris.

"Me too," said Julie. "The more women in business the better."

The French doors of the dining room were open, and a cool breeze from the ocean kept the room comfortable. For some reason there were fewer diners than on other nights. Velda and Nick were holding hands under the table and not being too discrete about it either. Judy and Myra weren't holding hands. I got the impression that they had had a falling out. Doris and Myra were engaged in a conversation about women journalists. Julie Patterson was pushing her food around her plate and not eating much at all.

"Something wrong with the food?" I asked her.

"No, the food is great. I'm just upset about my father. If he was really poisoned, there's only one person who could have done it. She lived with us for god's sake. I didn't care for her, but to think she could be so evil."

"We can't prove anything at this point and we'll need to hear back from the medical examiner. If she's guilty, I promise she will pay."

"What are you two whispering about over there?" asked Judy.

"Business," I said. "I'll explain later."

"Too much business talk if you ask me," replied Judy as she shot Myra a look.

"How long are you staying, Myra?" I asked because there had been a long silence at the table.

"Tomorrow I'm heading back to Boston," she answered. I figured that was the reason for the chill between her and Judy. "I need to start thinking of going back to Washington."

"Oh, how exciting," exclaimed Doris.

"Are you going back with her Judy?" I asked.

"Only as far as Boston."

"Indeed," sniffed Myra. "You know very well you're welcome to come to Washington with me."

"You should go, Judy." I was trying to encourage her. For some reason Judy hates Washington.

"Well, maybe," she said grudgingly.

"When are you leaving?" asked Velda looking at me.

"Hopefully in a day or two. I need to finish up some business with Julie."

"What about you and Nick?" I asked.

"Nick has another week off. As soon as I finish my painting of Mt. Cadillac we're going back to Monhegan for a few days and then back to Boston."

The waiter came over and handed me a piece of paper. "Telegram for you, sir," he said before he shuffled off. I read the telegram and put it away in my pocket.

"Bad news?" asked Velda.

"I'm not sure. Maybe, maybe not."

Chapter 29

Nick, Velda, and I were having coffee on the front porch of the hotel. The sky was clear and the smell of the ocean came over the gentle breeze. Later we would be seeing Myra and Judy off to the steamer for Portland where they would catch a train for Washington.

Nick and Velda were discussing their plans for the day while I was scanning the paper. It took me a while, but I found Doris Butler's gossip column.

> It seems, dear readers, that a certain lady real estate developer will be holding a private engagement party on Sunday evening at the house she is having built on Sunrise Hill. There is much speculation on just who the mystery man might be. A little bird told me that the house will be the future love nest.

"Excellent!" I said out loud.

"What's excellent?" asked Velda. I handed her the folded up paper with the gossip column.

"I hope this works," offered Nick.

"We'll see," I said as I got up to check on Judy and Myra's progress with packing.

With all the suitcases and trunks that Judy and Myra had there was hardly room in my car for the passengers. As it was I had to tie some of the luggage on the back of the car. Velda had excused herself to work on her painting, so it was just Nick and me that got to see them off.

"You'd think they were on an ocean voyage the way those two carry on," observed Nick as we watched the ship sail off.

"Judy loves drama. She watches so many movies that she thinks her life is like that of a movie star."

"I like them, just the same. I need to ask you something," Nick was looking uncomfortable.

"What is it?"

"It's about Velda."

"Yes?" I didn't know where this was going.

"I'm going to ask her to marry me."

"I see."

"I know what you're thinking. Cops don't make much money. But you see I come from a well-off family, and I do have a trust fund. I know you haven't known me for long but…"

"Stop, Nick, I'm not the one you have to convince. You need to ask Velda and she can be a handful. For my part I'd be happy to have you in the family. When are you going to ask her?"

"I'm taking her to town today for lunch."

"Well, good luck. She turned down Tommy Beckford last year, so don't get your hopes up. But right now I'm going to go see Julie Patterson. Want to ride along?"

"Of course."

"My phone has been ringing off the hook," said Julie as her receptionist ushered us into her office. "Everyone wants to know who my fiancé is."

"Hopefully the Jenkins boys will hear about it," added Nick.

"Oh, I have no doubt about that. Just to make sure I asked one of our mutual friends to let them know."

"Smart move," I agreed. "If they are going to do anything to the house before Sunday they either have to do it tonight or tomorrow. In either case Nick and I will be there."

"Be careful," she warned. "Those two can be dangerous."

"So can we," declared Nick with a little swagger.

It was late afternoon and I had just woken up from a nap when there was a knock at my door.

"Come in."

"Oh, Jeremy," cried Velda as she rushed into my room. "Nick has asked me to marry him." I could tell by the look on her face that she wasn't exactly unhappy about it.

"And?"

"I said yes."

211

"Congratulations," I said and stood up to kiss her. "I like Nick. He actually told me he was going to propose. I suppose he wanted my blessing."

"You must have given it to him."

"Indeed I did. I just want to make sure you thought about it carefully."

"I have. It just makes me uneasy that he's a policeman."

"Because?" I asked.

"Because he has a dangerous job. I'll worry every day."

"There's always a chance of danger regardless of work. Life is dangerous."

"Do you think I'm doing the right thing?"

"If you love him, and if you can't bear the thought of not seeing him every day, then you are doing the right thing."

We told the desk clerk that Nick and I were going hiking in Acadia National Park, and he had the kitchen pack us a thermos of coffee and some sandwiches. It promised to be a long night and Nick and I were ready to stake out the Sunrise Hill property and hopefully capture evidence to get the Jenkins boys arrested and convicted.

I had stopped at the sheriff's office to let him know what we were doing. Buck didn't have any men to spare for the stake out, but as a professional courtesy to Nick as a fellow officer, he loaned us two guns and some handcuffs.

"You both be careful," warned Velda as we left for the night. "Take a blanket so you don't have to sit on the cold ground."

As soon as the sun began setting I drove the car toward Sunrise Hill and parked it out of sight in a wooded side road. We hiked in the quarter mile and set up camp in some shrubs where we had a good view of the house.

"Wish we had a radio," sighed Nick.

"A battery set would be too heavy to carry very far."

"What was in that telegram you got last night?" asked Nick changing the subject. "If you don't mind my asking."

"It was from Rob. It seems that Mildred Blasdell, Ina Patterson's house guest, died of an accidental overdose of her sleeping medicine."

"Accidental?"

"That's the report. It seems like a pattern is emerging."

"And of course, there's no way to determine that Ina slipped her the medicine."

"Not yet, but I'm determined to put her away."

"And," whispered Nick looking toward the house as two figures appeared, "it may not be a long night after all."

Chapter 30

The moon was only half full so it didn't provide a lot of light, but it was enough to see two shadowy figures lurking near the house. They had boldly parked their Ford pickup truck figuring this was an isolated spot.

"What are they doing now?" I asked Nick as he was watching through a pair of binoculars.

"Assholes are drinking beer. Must need to get their courage up."

"Not much we can do until they actually try to start a fire. They could just claim they were checking the place out."

"The trick is to catch them making fire before they burn the place down."

I reached for my gun and made sure that it was loaded and ready to go. Nick put down the binoculars and did the same.

"First sign of fire, we move in," I whispered to Nick.

"Let's get closer," Nick said as he moved toward the house in the darkness. I kept an eye on our suspects to make sure they didn't see us. "That's funny."

"What's funny?" I asked in a whisper.

"There something strange about the second guy."

I looked but didn't see anything unusual. I took up the binoculars, but in the dark they weren't much help. We got closer. Nick hid behind one tree and I hid behind another. The good thing about the

214

dark is it would make it easier to spot a fire. It didn't take long before we saw a match flare up and a small fire ignite. I stepped out from behind the tree and pointed my gun at the offenders. Nick did the same.

"Stop right there," I said. "Put the flame out." They stomped out the small fire. "Now put your hands in the air where I can see them."

As Nick and I closed in I could see what Nick meant about something funny. The taller man had a hat on that kept his face in the dark. The second figure was slight with long hair. I took the flashlight for a closer look.

"You're a girl!" I said surprised by what I saw. I turned the flashlight onto the other face. "And you're Buddy Levesque."

"I thought you said Julie Patterson was not in competition with you," Nick said as he reached for the handcuffs."

"Bitch stole my work. I'd be the one building the houses if she hadn't taken over her old man's business."

A thought struck me. "You killed old man Patterson, didn't you? You poisoned him and then pushed his car over the edge of the road."

"You can't prove anything."

"I can prove that you've been starting the fires. And no, I can't prove that you killed old man Patterson. But I'm guessing that this young lady is your daughter. Be a pity to send her off to jail. How old are you, sweetie?" I asked.

"I'm sixteen," she said in a frightened voice.

"Let's see," said Nick as he shoved Buddy Levesque up against the truck. "You've given drink to a minor in your care and you've involved her in a crime. I'll bet her mother isn't going to be pleased about any of this."

"Let her go!" Levesque said in a pleading voice. I looked over at the young girl and she was shivering from fear.

"Maybe we'll make a deal," I offered. "Tell us the truth and we'll talk about letting her go. What's your name, honey?"

"Martha," she said. She was in tears now, and I felt very sorry for her. Whatever the outcome was going to be, her life was about to change.

"You're right. I killed the old man, just let her go. She didn't do anything."

"Just to make sure you're not lying to save your daughter," questioned Nick, "what did you poison him with?"

"I invited him to have a beer with me. I laced the beer with cocaine."

"We'll see if the coroner agrees with you," I said. "Now let's get you to the sheriff's office."

"What about my daughter?" Levesque whined.

"You're in no position to make any deals now," said Nick and held the gun on him.

"I'll bring the car around. Looks like we're all taking a ride."

"I can't believe any of this," said Julie Patterson the next day when Nick and I went to call on her. "You had me convinced that Ina killed him."

"I was sure she was guilty, but the coroner confirmed that he died of a cocaine overdose," I replied.

"This doesn't help out your case at all, does it?" she asked me.

"No, it doesn't. I'm no closer now to proving or disproving her guilt in the deaths of her first two husbands."

"What's going to happen to the girl?"

"We took her home to her mother," said Nick. "The mother promised to take care of the girl. It seems Mrs. Levesque had left her husband quite a while back. He was using the girl to get back at his wife."

"You've really helped me out," said Julie. "What do I owe you?"

"Nothing," I answered. "You never hired me. I was here trying to nail Ina Patterson. As it happens, she is innocent of this one."

I offered to drive Nick and Velda to Port Clyde to catch the mail boat for Monhegan, but they said they preferred to take the steamer to Rockland. I suspected they were eager to be alone.

I loaded up the car and headed out of Bar Harbor. I had helped stop an arsonist and uncovered a murder, but neither had helped me

217

solve a case I'd been on since the beginning of summer. My plans for a quiet summer in the White Mountains of New Hampshire seemed to be slipping away.

Chapter 31

As soon as I drove away from the coast and over the New Hampshire border I was hit with hot humid air that made me wish I'd stayed in Bar Harbor. The roads were crowded mostly by people heading north away from Boston. Riding along I had some time to think. I had struck out trying to prove that Ina Patterson didn't kill her third husband, but that didn't clear her of the other deaths.

Two husbands with heart attacks and a house guest with an accidental overdose of sleeping medicine still looked suspicious to me. Nora Wilde was looking to me to stop the marriage of her father and Ina, but I wasn't sure I could.

I contemplated telling her I couldn't continue the case, but I wanted to give it one more try.

Roscoe met me at the door and took the car keys to put the car away. Rob was at work so I decided to invite Nora Wilde for lunch. Even though the Parker House was not far away from my Beacon Hill townhouse, it was difficult walking in the heat.

I was taken to a table in the corner and ordered a gin and tonic while I waited for Nora. I saw her enter the room and look around. When she spotted me she came over.

"I hope this lunch isn't going on my expense tab," she said smiling.

"You're expense tab is so large it wouldn't make much difference."

"What are you drinking?" she asked.

"Gin and tonic."

She flagged down the waiter and ordered the same. "What is it you want to tell me?

I gave her the story of what had transpired in Bar Harbor. I could tell she was disappointed.

"Well, it sounds like you did good work, but it doesn't really help me does it now?"

"No, it does not. I'm not charging you for the time at Bar Harbor, but I seem to be running out of options. So I need to know if you want me to continue, knowing that I might not be able to prove Ina is guilty of anything."

"If nothing else she's a gold digger. I want you to continue. I've brought my check book along. How much so far?"

I gave her the numbers, and she didn't even flinch. I took the check. They say money doesn't buy happiness. I say bull shit.

"I'll write up a report about what I've found out so far about Ina. You can decide whether to give it to your father or not. Chances are he won't believe it and will be angry with you for trying to interfere. But hold off for a few days and let me see if I can dig something else up."

"May I take your order now?" asked the waiter.

"Yes," said Nora. "I think we are ready."

When I got back from lunch Rob was waiting for me. I realized he didn't know about what had transpired in Bar Harbor. Neither did Roscoe, so I had them sit down while I told them about finding the arsonist and that he turned out to be the Patterson killer.

"Damn, I always miss the good stuff," exclaimed Roscoe. "I leave you on your own and you go around solving stuff."

"And," I continued, "Nick Liberty has asked Velda to marry him."

"I wasn't expecting that," said Rob.

"Me, either," I said. "I suppose we'll have to wait for a formal announcement."

"Well, I have some news that may help your case. It seems that Ina's houseguest Mildred Blasdell, made Ina the beneficiary of her estate," Rob looked like he was enjoying my surprise.

"There's no doubt in my mind now that she's guilty," I said.

"But," Rob reminded me, "you have to prove it."

"I know. I think I'll make a call on Mrs. Patterson. I'll need to take Emma Goodwin along."

I phoned Emma Goodwin and told her I'd pick her up in an hour. She protested that an hour didn't give her enough time to get ready, so I gave her an hour and a half. I called for her at the agreed time, and she appeared with a strikingly large black hat and an equally large purse. I helped her into the car and drove along to Ina's place.

"Are you sure you're going to be comfortable in the heat?" I asked. Thinking the hat may be too much.

"Jeremy, I've lived through more summers than you can imagine. Don't worry about me. Now remember, your name is Van Clef, not Dance."

"That's good," I replied, "because as it happens a private detective named Dance solved the mystery of her late husband's death."

"You did what?"

I told her about the arsonist and killer and how I was disappointed not to have found out for sure if she was a murderess or not.

"You heard about poor Miss Blasdell?" she asked.

"Yes, I did. And I just learned that she signed everything over to Ina before her unfortunate accident."

"Too many coincidences in her story for me to believe she's innocent," said Emma.

We pulled up in front of Ina's Brookline house, and I helped Emma out of the car. Ina Patterson must have seen us drive up because she came out to greet us.

"Mrs. Goodwin and Mr. Van Clef, what a treat. Come in out of the heat." Ina led us into a small parlor that was much cooler than the rest of the house. The windows were open and looked out over a shaded garden. We were seated and lemonade was sent for.

"We came to see how you're doing, dear," cooed Emma. "What a shock to find out that your husband Bruce was murdered.

"I'm still in shock," replied Ina, but her face reflected some other emotion. "The sheriff in Bar Harbor called me yesterday and told me about that awful man. Imagine my poor Bruce murdered!"

I wasn't buying the play acting and neither was Emma, I could tell.

"I was sorry to hear about poor Miss Blasdell, too," I said.

"Oh, yes," sighed Ina. "Poor thing was so forgetful. She must have taken her sleeping potion absentmindedly."

"Sure, that's it," I said under my breath. Emma gave me a discrete kick.

"I must find this detective and thank him. I always suspected that my stepdaughter Julie held me responsible for his accident. Hopefully she'll see that I had nothing to do with it.

"So," said Emma to change the subject, "you must be counting the days until your marriage."

"I had planned to make it sooner. After all why waste time at my age. But his daughter Nora convinced him to have it in the fall when it's cooler. They have relations coming in from all over the country."

Something wasn't right. She was talking too fast and her voice was too high pitched. Her smile was friendly, but her eyes weren't. Then it hit me. She knew that Jeremy Van Clef was in reality

Jeremy Dance. She was afraid. I decided to take the advantage.

"Funny thing about this Levesque guy," I said. "He doesn't seem smart enough to murder your husband. Almost like someone planned it out for him. It's interesting that he drives a brand new Ford truck, top of the line. He didn't get that on the money he made from house repairs."

"Who would do that?"

"You'll have to forgive Jeremy, my dear. He's been reading too many cheap novels." Emma was trying to defuse the tension in the air. I wasn't done with her yet. If she knew who I really was there was no point in trying to hide it now.

"You have the most beautiful flowers,' I said getting up and going to the side table where a bouquet of fresh cut flowers had been placed in an art deco vase. "Are these from your garden?"

"Yes, they are."

And then I noticed what type of flowers they were and suddenly I knew how she killed her husbands. "These are beautiful foxgloves. Did you know that digitalis, a heart medicine, comes from foxglove? Too much of it, though can bring on a heart attack."

I was turned away from her, but out of the corner of my eye I saw her grab an iron poker from the fireplace and raise her arm. I spun around to stop her but a shot rang out, there was a scream, and Ina Patterson crumpled to the ground.

I looked up in surprise to see Emma Goodwin holding a pistol, looking cool as a cucumber.

"Ina, dear," said Emma, "That's no way to treat your guests."

Chapter 32

Velda and Nick invited us to dinner to celebrate their engagement. They had only been back for a day and hadn't heard all the details of my story. It was a festive dinner with Rob and me and several of Velda and Nick's friends. We were on our second round of cocktails.

"Was she badly hurt?" asked Tommy Beckford, who didn't look at all happy to be celebrating Velda's engagement.

"Just a flesh wound to the leg. It was enough to slow her down," I replied.

"So she confessed?" asked Nick.

"Ina refused to say anything when the police arrived. I called the Hancock County sheriff and told him I suspected that Levesque had been paid off. He spilled the beans on Ina when he realized he could make a deal."

"What about the other husbands?" asked Velda.

"There's no way to prove that she killed them, but no need as she'll be tried for the murder of Bruce Patterson in Maine. There is an interesting twist to the story, however."

"What's that?" asked one of the guests whose name was Maggie.

"I convinced Nora Wilde to look closer into the death of her mother. Her father, of course, was stunned that his soon-to-be bride was a murderess. But they've ordered an exhumation of the mother. I'm guessing that she didn't die of natural causes?"

"Digitalis?" asked Velda.

"Oh, yes. I think it's probable that Ina was on the train to New York with Nora's mother and slipped her a digitalis laced drink."

"Good work, Jeremy," said Nick Liberty.

"What was she planning to do once she conked you on the head?" asked Tommy. I suspected his interest in the crime was his way of not thinking about Velda with another man.

"I think she was in a panic and was going to try to run away. She wasn't too worried about Emma running after her," I explained.

"Imagine that sweet old lady with a gun," said Velda.

"That sweet old lady," I replied, "is one tough broad."

The door bell rang and Velda bolted out of her seat to answer the door.

"What was all that about?" I asked. Nick shrugged his shoulders. Velda came into the room with an older gentleman following her. He was about my height with graying hair and close to sixty.

"Dad!" I said in surprise.

"Your sister invited me to celebrate her engagement. Might I have a private word with you son?"

I hesitated for a moment caught completely by surprise. Rob practically pushed me out of my seat. "Okay," I said and led him into Velda's writing room.

"Before you say anything," said my father holding up his hand, "I've got something to say."

I looked at him and said nothing.

"I've been a fool, and I've treated you badly. I let that woman have too much control over my life. I've come to ask your forgiveness."

"Is she really gone?" I asked feeling like a ten year old again.

"She's gone for good. You and Velda are the most important people in my life. I'm sorry that I forgot that."

To my utter surprise, I reached out and gave him a hug.

The End

THE AUTHOR

Stephen E. Stanley grew up on the Maine coast and graduated from Morse High School in Bath. He attended the University of Southern Maine, Lesley University, the University of New Hampshire, and Columbia Pacific University.

Mr. Stanley was a high school educator for over thirty years and recently retired as the district mentor for secondary education at a large New Hampshire school system.